The Bad Luck Chair

SUE WILKOWSKI

ILLUSTRATED BY
CB DECKER

Dutton
Children's
Books

For Hannah, Mia, and Brian
with love

Dutton Children's Books

A division of Penguin Young Readers Group

Published by the Penguin Group / Penguin Group (USA) Inc., 375 Hudson Street, New York, New York 10014, U.S.A. / Penguin Group (Canada), 90 Eglinton Avenue East, Suite 700, Toronto, Ontario, Canada M4P 2Y3 (a division of Pearson Penguin Canada Inc.) / Penguin Books Ltd, 80 Strand, London WC2R 0RL, England / Penguin Ireland, 25 St Stephen's Green, Dublin 2, Ireland (a division of Penguin Books Ltd) / Penguin Group (Australia), 250 Camberwell Road, Camberwell, Victoria 3124, Australia (a division of Pearson Australia Group Pty Ltd) / Penguin Books India Pvt Ltd, 11 Community Centre, Panchsheel Park, New Delhi - 110 017, India / Penguin Group (NZ), 67 Apollo Drive, Rosedale, North Shore 0745, Auckland, New Zealand (a division of Pearson New Zealand Ltd) / Penguin Books (South Africa) (Pty) Ltd, 24 Sturdee Avenue, Rosebank, Johannesburg 2196, South Africa / Penguin Books Ltd, Registered Offices: 80 Strand, London WC2R 0RL, England

The publisher does not have any control over and does not assume any responsibility for author or third-party websites or their content.

CIP Data is available.

Published in the United States by Dutton Children's Books,
a division of Penguin Young Readers Group, 345 Hudson Street, New York, New York 10014
www.penguin.com/youngreaders

DESIGNED BY HEATHER WOOD
Printed in USA / First Edition
ISBN: 978-0-525-47794-5 / 10 9 8 7 6 5 4 3 2 1

Contents

The Bad Luck Chair

Sit Down!

1

Addison Darby stepped into her classroom and stopped short. Something was going on. Something big. Kids were crowded around her spot. They were pushing and shoving and stretching their necks to get a good look at—Addy wasn't sure what. But she *was* sure that whatever it was, it was sitting in *her* seat.

"*Look, she's here,*" Addy heard someone whisper. A few kids pointed. The rest of her classmates turned toward her and stared.

Addy felt frozen. Glued to the ground. She was stuck in place right inside Room 36. Kids who still needed to come in had to turn sideways and squeeze past.

Why is everyone standing by my desk? she asked herself. *Why are they all staring at ME?*

"Bad news, Addy," said Sam, Addy's best friend. Kids moved out of the way so she could see him. He was right next to her desk.

"B-bad news? What is it, Sam? What's going on?" She shoved her hands deep into her coat pockets and took a half step back.

"Here's the thing," Sam began. "It's *bad* bad, Addy. So I'm just going to say it. Okay?"

"O-okay." Addy was terrified. Not only from wondering what the *bad* bad news could be, but also because the whole class was watching her as she stood there wondering.

"It's The Chair," Sam said softly.

"Wh-what?" Addy's ears had heard what Sam had said. Loud and clear. But her brain didn't want to believe it.

"The Chair is at your desk." Sam pointed to it.

Addy looked. She felt sweaty and gaggy. The bad thing wasn't *in* her chair. The bad thing *was* her chair. It was *The Chair.*

The Brookside Elementary Bad Luck Chair!

Every kid in every classroom knew about it. Its legend was passed from friend to friend, old-timer to newcomer, busser to walker. Even if you were lucky enough never to have seen it, you knew what it looked like. Every kid did.

Its top left corner was chipped, and one leg was slime green. The dark, dreadful stain on its seat was shaped like a skull. And it had initials carved deep into its back. Bad Luck initials. B.L.

It was a chair that cursed every kid in its path.

A chair whose path no kid could cross.

"Let's get a move on, people," Ms. Stern called, clapping her hands. "We have a busy day ahead of us." She glanced at Addy and added, "Addison, why are you standing in the doorway?"

Addy felt every eyeball in the room zoom in on her again. With everyone watching, her mouth forgot how to make words. "Um, I, uh . . ."

"Well, it's time to start our day, Addison," Ms. Stern cut in. She sat at her desk and opened her attendance book.

Addy gripped the straps of her backpack so her hands wouldn't shake. She went to Ms. Stern's desk. Softly, with her back to the class, she asked, "Can I have a different ch-chair, Ms. Stern? Mine's, uh, not a good one. Someone put it there." Addy turned her head and pointed her chin toward The Chair.

Ms. Stern looked at it, then back at Addy. "The school furniture was inspected this weekend," Ms. Stern explained. "It was time for the mid-year safety check. Your old chair probably needed to be repaired, Addison. So the custodians took it away and replaced it with a different one from storage. A chair's a chair," she added. "Hang up your coat, unpack your backpack, then go *sit in it*."

Sam came up to stand next to Addy. "But Ms. Stern," he urged, "it's chipped, and one leg is green."

"It's fine, Samuel."

"Ms. Stern?" Brittney called from her seat near the front.

"Yes, Brittney?"

"You see, there's a problem," Brittney said. Her voice sounded sweeter than a mouthful of cotton candy. And as fake as a battery-operated dog that barks and wags its tail. Brittney flashed a mean smile at Addy.

Addy thought Brittney was as scary as The Chair.

"What's the problem?" Ms. Stern asked.

"The problem," Brittney began, "is that Addison thinks that chair is The Bad Luck Chair." She rolled her eyes and added, "Addison thinks terrible things will happen to her if she sits in it."

Addy was furious. She wished she had enough guts to tell Brittney to stop barging in on *private* conversations. To tell Brittney to shut her mouth and mind her own business. To stop acting like she was the second teacher in the room.

But Addy didn't have enough guts. She didn't have *any* guts. So instead, she said nothing.

"Is *that* what this is all about?" Ms. Stern asked. "That's silly!" She waved the idea away with her hand. "There is no such thing as a bad luck chair."

Addy felt like a bowling ball had hit her in the stomach.

"The two of you need to move along," Ms. Stern said to Addy and Sam. "It's Monday morning and we have to get to work." She stood, took a piece of chalk from the ledge, and began to write the week's spelling words on the board.

"*There is too such a thing,*" Sam mumbled.

Ms. Stern stopped writing. She turned back around. "Did you have something to say, Samuel?" she asked. "Speak up," she went on, her voice sounding stormier with each word. "I'm sure the whole class would like to hear!"

Sam blinked two times. Addy knew that meant he was scared. Sam always blinked when he got scared.

"I said that . . . there *is* such a thing as The Bad Luck Chair."

"Is that so, Samuel?" Ms. Stern asked.

"Yuh-huh." Blink, blink. "You probably don't know about it because this is your first year at Brookside," he replied. "But *that chair* really is The Bad Luck Chair."

Brittney laughed just loud enough for Addy to hear, just low enough to be sure Ms. Stern didn't.

Ms. Stern put her hands on her hips.

"The legend says that a long time ago there was this kid named Bart Levit," Sam began. "Bart had black hair and gold eyes and ate live bugs for lunch. And he wore the same shirt to school every day. It was brown and it had silver hexagon buttons." Sam drew a hexagon in the air with his finger. "Bart liked hanging around the old cemetery across from the park," Sam went on. "Kids saw him there all the time. After school, on weekends. Sometimes even at night. Then one day, Bart disappeared. Just like that, he was gone. And he never came back. Well actually, not *never*. Six weeks after he disappeared," Sam explained, his voice lower, "kids walked into their classroom, and sitting on the seat of Bart's old chair was a button. One silver hexagon button. And carved into the back of the chair were his initials: B.L. Some say Bart wasn't really a kid—he was a ghost. No one knows for sure. But everyone knows that Bart came back for one last visit and cursed his chair. He made it The Bad Luck Chair. And since that day, anyone who sits in it gets cursed with bad luck."

The class was so still that Addy was sure she could hear Sam blink.

"Well," Ms. Stern said, jolting the kids from the quiet. "I must say you have a vivid imagination, Samuel. That will come in handy for our creative writing workshop. But for now, it's time to get to work!"

"But Ms. Stern," Sam said, "there's proof! Ben Melman, the math brain, failed a test the day he sat in The Chair. He failed it so bad he lost his chance to be in the Brookside Math Olympics!"

Kids nodded hard. Their moving heads made Addy dizzy.

"The day Olivia Brown sat in The Chair," Sam went on, "she tripped in her dance class. She broke her toe and couldn't dance in her recital. The dance teacher had to give her solo to another dancer!"

The class gasped. Addy felt the air in the room get sucked away. She was woozy and wobbly.

And then words were spoken so softly, Addy wasn't sure if she heard them or imagined them.

"My brother sat in The Chair."

Addy turned to Katie O., the quiet girl in the back.

"My brother sat in The Chair," Katie O. said again, just as softly.

"H-he did?" Addy said back.

"Yup."

"When?" Sam asked.

"A while ago. Before Ben and Olivia."

"Is he o-okay?" Addy asked, though she wasn't sure she wanted to know the answer.

Katie shook her head. "Nope, he's not okay. It was *way* bad. He was a fourth-grader then, like us," she explained. "He's in eighth grade now, at the middle school. Never got over what The Chair did to him."

"R-really?"

"*Way* really."

"That's it," Ms. Stern said. "Enough is enough. Katie, I'd like you to stop talking about this *right now*. And Addy, I'm sorry that you think something is wrong with your chair. I'll put in an order for another one later today. But for now, you need to go sit down in it."

Addy *did* need to sit down. But she needed a chair to sit down in. One that didn't make math brains flunk. One that didn't make solo dancers trip. One that didn't do whatever *"way* bad" thing it had done to Katie O.'s brother.

"I think," Addy said, holding the corner of Ms. Stern's desk to steady herself, "I think I need to g-go to the nurse."

"I think what everyone needs is to take their seats and copy this week's spelling words," Ms. Stern snapped. "It's time to be busy birds and get going!"

"B-but Ms. Stern . . ."

"ADDISON, SIT DOWN NOW!"

The Triangle Note

2

Addy already had a history of bad luck with chairs.

In first grade, her shoelace got caught in the leg of her seat and she fell flat on her face. Her nose turned black and blue, and her lip looked swollen and lopsided. But that wasn't the worst part. The worst part was that class picture day was the very *next* day. So while all of her class-mates looked smiley and picture perfect, Addy looked like a weird fish. The kind you see on TV shows called *The World's Most Unusual Creatures*.

In third grade, Addy's chair problems got worse. She sat down in the cafeteria at the end of the day to wait for her bus number to be called. She didn't see the sign that had fallen off the wall and landed face down on her chair. Or the sticky tape on the back of that sign. But when her bus number was called and she got up, everyone behind her saw it. Because the sign had taped itself to the seat of her pants. It read: BUS DUTY. She could still hear kids teasing her about it.

"Ew. Addy made doody on the bus."

"Addy didn't make it to the bathroom in time after she rode the bus."

"Addy sat in doody. Addy sat in doody."

Addy was horrified. Mortified. Miserable. It was the most embarrassing thing that had ever happened to her in her whole life. She didn't think the teasing would ever stop. So, like Herman, her pet hermit crab, she crawled into a shell. Not a beautiful striped one like Herman's. An imaginary one. And while she was in it, Addy hardly ever spoke up in class and never ever did *anything* to call attention to herself. Before long, kids didn't notice that she was in the room. Which, Addy thought, was a good thing, because they also didn't bother to tease her. Addy sometimes felt invisible, but most of the time she felt safe and comfortable, like Herman.

Until The Chair showed up tucked nice and neat under her desk. And, just like that, it was as if she had been outlined with a neon-pink highlighter. *Hey, everyone, look over here at Addison Darby,* the highlighter screamed. *Don't take your eyes off Addy!*

Addy walked from Ms. Stern's desk to the back of the room, right behind Sam. When they got there, she dropped her backpack and took off her winter gloves.

"I'm in Troubleville, Sam," she whispered. "Major Troubleville."

"I know," he answered. He hung his coat on his peg.

"Everyone is staring at me," Addy went on.

"I know," he said again. "But they don't mean to. If someone else found The Chair, we'd probably be staring, too. Not in a bad way. Just in a, ya know, staring way."

Addy knew Sam was right. Still, she felt uneasy. She hung up her coat and stowed her things in her bin.

"Maybe Ms. Stern will ask the custodians for another chair this morning," Sam tried.

"But they just gave me this one," Addy replied. "They're not going to think anything's wrong with it. So there's no way they're going to take it back and give me a different one."

Sam nodded. "Then what are you gonna do?" he asked.

"No know," Addy answered. It was what they always said to each other when they got stuck on puzzles. Addy and Sam *loved* word puzzles. It was their favorite thing to do. They even started a club called The Word Nerds. They were the only two members, and they met every week.

"I know what I *can't* do," Addy said. "I can't sit in The Chair."

"For real, you can't sit in it," Sam agreed. "For supreme real. That thing's scary."

"Eh-hem." Ms. Stern cleared her throat. Addy knew that *Eh-hem* meant *I'm watching you* in Ms. Stern language.

"I think we have to go to our . . . seats," Sam said, looking around. Most of the kids in the class already had their spelling notebooks out. Sam shrugged a sad, helpless shrug, then went to his seat.

And Addy began to move slowly toward hers. She didn't know which was worse, seeing all the heads in the room turn to watch her walk to her desk, or seeing The Chair waiting for her when she got there. It was a long, hard journey. Step by step, it got worse and worse.

"If I were you I'd fake faint," Melissa said when Addy finally got to her desk. Melissa sat next to her, in their group.

"You'd wh-what?" Addy asked.

"I'd like, fake faint," Melissa repeated. She took a wipe from the container in her desk and cleaned her hands with it. "Actually, I'd real faint if I really had to sit *there*." She gazed at The Chair, then covered her eyes. "I feel spooked just looking at it!"

"Ms. Stern would know she's faking," Hillary argued. Hillary was in their group, too. Her desk faced Addy's and Melissa's, touching the middle of both. "Maybe you should try to sit like you're using a bathroom in the mall," Hillary went on. "You know, when you sit without touching the seat." She pretended, using her own chair.

Addy thought she looked uncomfortable.

"I hate to break it to you, but she couldn't sit that way all day," Melissa pointed out.

Ms. Stern cleared her throat. "If you have not already begun to copy this week's words, begin right now," she commanded.

Addy checked around the room. Soon she would be the only one standing.

"*Psst*, Hillary," Melissa called in a loud whisper. "It's easier to use liners."

"Liners?" Hillary fell from her bathroom sit to a regular sit. "What are *liners*?" she asked.

"Toilet-seat liners," Melissa answered. "They're sheets of paper you put on the toilet. That way you don't touch the seat when you, ya know, *go*. Like in the mall. Or here. These bathrooms are disgusting. I always carry a few."

Even though Melissa and Hillary always talked, talked, talked, Addy could not believe they were talking about dirty bathrooms and toilet-seat liners right in the middle of her Chair Emergency. Until their conversation gave her an idea. "Melissa," she whispered, "do you think those liners would work for me?"

Melissa shrugged and asked back, "Like, why wouldn't they?"

"N-not to put on the toilet. To put here." Addy pointed. "On The Chair."

"Stop the chatting and take your seat now, Addison!" Ms. Stern picked up her grade book. She took a red pen

out of the bird penholder that sat on her desk, then wrote
something down. In all of Addy's school years, she had
never, not once, gotten a red mark next to her name in a
black book.

It was all because of The Chair. And she hadn't even sat
in it yet!

"Here," Melissa mouthed. She handed a neatly folded
toilet-seat liner to Addy.

The second Addy had the liner in her hand, she realized
it could lead to trouble. Anything at all to do with bathrooms could remind kids of the Bus Duty thing. She closed
her hand around it and hoped no one knew what it was.

Ms. Stern's back was to the class. Addy ducked under
her desk and unfolded the liner.

Ms. Stern turned back around. "Addison!" she shouted. "What are you doing *now*?"

"Uh, uh, I'm uh . . ."

"She's finding her pencil," Melissa answered. "It dropped."

Addy hid the liner behind her back. She stayed put under her desk.

"Find it. Sit. Write!" Ms. Stern shouted.

Ms. Stern only talked like a robot when she got really mad. She'd never spoken to Addy like that before. Before The Chair.

Without looking at the skull stain, which was looking right at her, Addy dropped the liner onto the seat. She got out from under her desk. And she did what she had to do. With everyone in the whole class watching, she sat.

Addison Darby sat in The Bad Luck Chair.

It was hard work. Addy had to stay perfectly still. She couldn't allow her back to touch its back, or her legs to touch its legs. She hoped that if she didn't bother The Chair, The Chair wouldn't bother her. And if The Chair didn't bother her, maybe no one else would, either.

Every Chair minute felt like a month. Addy tried to listen to Ms. Stern's science lesson on buoyancy. She folded her paper in half the long way, like Ms. Stern had said to do. And she tried to list things that *float* on the left side of the crease, and things that *sink* on the right. But instead, she imagined taking The Chair to the brook that was right beside Brookside Elementary. She pictured herself flinging The Chair in and watching it struggle to stay above water. Then, in her mind, she saw it bobble one last time before it sank. She thought about how good that would feel. How much fun it would be to write *The Chair* on the *sink* side of her list. Even Ms. Stern could not expect her to sit in a chair that sat on the bottom of a brook.

"Addy!" Ms. Stern called out. "Stop daydreaming and get to work!"

When lunchtime finally rolled around, Addy's back ached, her legs were limp, and her bottom felt numb. But she rose from that seat like she'd done it a million times before. Nothing touched. Addy hadn't brushed it, hadn't skimmed it, hardly even sat in it.

"I did it, Sam! I sat in The Chair without touching it!" They walked to the lunchroom together.

"For real, you did it," he said. "I bet you set some sort of record. You should get into the Brookside Hall of Fame. First person ever to survive a whole morning of The Chair."

"Maybe I should," Addy agreed.

Addy and Sam sat across from each other in their usual lunch spots. Addy pulled a sandwich from her bag. Out came a soggy, squishy blob. "*Ewww*. My drink leaked all over everything."

Sam looked at Addy. "You think . . ."

"What? Think what?"

"You think that your wet sandwich is . . . because of, uh, The Chair?" Sam asked.

Addy looked at the wet bread. "Probably," she answered. "Even though I didn't touch The Chair, I was *near* it. I guess being near it is enough to make bad things happen. Maybe not terrible things at first." She dropped the gooey sandwich back into her damp lunch bag. "But it'll probably get worse."

"Much worse," Sam agreed. He gave her half of his turkey and pickle sandwich.

"Hey, Addy," Brittney called from the other end of the lunch table. She was giggling with a few of her friends. "Here," she said. "Catch!" She threw a paper airplane. It came in for a perfect landing on the table right in front of Addy.

"Open it up!" Brittney urged, loud enough for the whole class to hear. "I know you like word games. I made one up *just for you.*"

Addy didn't want to, but everyone was watching. She opened up the plane and flattened it out. It said:

WORD SCRAMBLE
USB ODOYD

Addy felt a cry start to push its way up and out. She crumpled up the plane while Brittney and her friends laughed at her.

"What am I gonna do, Sam?" Addy asked. "All of this is because of The Chair. I gotta think of a way to get rid of it!"

"For *supreme real* you have to get rid of The Chair. That thing scares the crackers out of me," Sam replied. "But with Ms. Stern and her beady bird eyes watching you, I don't know how."

"Me neither."

They returned to class. Addy dragged herself back to her spot. There she found a perfectly folded triangle note waiting on her desk. She figured it was just another mean one from Brittney. But then she saw that her name was written with a green marker, not a blue pen like the one Brittney had used. And the handwriting looked different, too. Addy decided to open it. It read:

I have secret information that can help you. Meet me by the swings after school.

Katie O.

Lucky

3

"They used to call my brother Lucky," Katie began. She wore purple polka-dot gloves. Her hat had little purple pom-poms all over it instead of one big one in the middle. Addy wasn't surprised. Katie O. always dressed a little wild that way.

Addy was nervous. She wasn't used to talking with kids she didn't really know. "Who's th-they?" she asked.

"Everyone," Katie answered. "Friends. Cousins. Even his teachers. They called him Lucky 'cause that's what he was. *Lucky.*"

Addy dropped her backpack onto the ground and sat in the swing next to Katie's.

"Like when he put a quarter in a gum-ball machine,"

Katie went on, "he got green every time." She pushed her swing to make it move a little.

"Green?" Addy pushed her swing, too. It was ice-cold out, so there were hardly any kids in the schoolyard. Addy was glad. Chair news had spread and kids had been pointing at her all day.

"Yup, green. His favorite. And whenever he played bingo," Katie continued, "he'd win. Across, diagonal, corners only. Even blackout bingo. If a number was on his card, it got called."

"Sounds like he lived in Luckyville," Addy said.

"Lived there? He was *king* of the place!"

Addy was surprised at how loud Katie was talking. In class she always spoke softly, if at all. They were both the same that way.

"My brother used to be so lucky, so, so, *so* lucky," Katie went on, "that one time he walked through the doors of Ivan's Ice Cream World and won free ice cream for a whole year!"

"Just for walking in?"

"Yup. He walked in and the whole place went gaga! Bells started ringing and lights started flashing. And all the people who worked there started blowing whistles!"

Addy stopped her swing. "All he did was walk in?"

"He was the five thousandth person to walk in," Katie explained. She stopped her swing, too. "Do you wanna hear the best part?"

"There's more?"

"Way more!"

Addy couldn't imagine anything better than winning free ice cream for a year. "Okay."

"Ivan named a flavor after him."

"Wow! Which one?"

"Lucky's Lick Your Lips Lime," Katie answered, her tongue darting out like a lizard's at every *L*. "Green ice cream with green jelly beans and green gum balls all mixed in."

Addy knew that flavor. She never picked it because she didn't like lime. But she'd heard that it was named after some kid in town. At that very moment, Addy knew that Katie O. was telling the truth. Under her heavy winter coat, hoodie, and long-sleeved tee, Addy felt goose bumps pop out all over. She had never known anyone even half as lucky as Lucky.

"Uh, Katie?" she began.

"Nope," Katie answered fast, before Addy could ask. "He's not lucky anymore. He's *unlucky* now. Sat in The Chair and BAM, his good luck turned to bad." She kicked the hard, cold ground with the heel of her sneaker. "Do you wanna hear the worst part?"

Not really, Addy thought. Her brain felt full, too full, the way her stomach sometimes felt when she ate one hot dog too many. She shrugged.

"He sat in The Chair on a dare. *On a dare*," Katie repeated. "That's the worst part of the whole thing. It's not like he sat in it by accident, or because some teacher made him. He knew all about The Chair. But he wasn't scared of it. He figured anyone named Lucky couldn't get beat up by The Bad Luck Chair."

"He, uh, figured wrong?"

"Way! He figured way, way wrong. He sat in The Chair one time. Sat, counted to twenty-eight, which was his lucky number, then got up. Now, if he puts a quarter in a gumball machine, he loses the quarter and doesn't get a gumball. If he plays bingo, his numbers never get called. And every time he walks into Ivan's, they're out of his flavor."

Addy knew that if someone as special as Katie's brother could be chewed up and spit back out in twenty-eight seconds flat, she didn't stand a chance. She stood up, picked up her backpack, and swung it onto her shoulder. "I thought the *secret information* you had was good, Katie. Your note said that it could help me." Addy shoved her hands into her pockets and added, "Sorry about your brother. Really. But now I feel worse than I did before." She turned and walked toward the gate.

"Wait!" Katie called, and ran after her. "There's more!"

Addy stopped and turned around. "There is?"

"The secret information is how to *reverse the curse* of The Bad Luck Chair," Katie said.

"Wow! How to *reverse the curse*? That's great!"

Katie nodded.

"But wait a minute," Addy said, thinking out loud. "If your brother knows how to reverse the curse, why hasn't he reversed it already?"

"Because," Katie answered, "the secret information is still, er, sort of a secret."

Addy looked toward the gate, then back to Katie. "I don't get it," she said.

"It's complicated," Katie explained. "My brother worked really hard to figure it out. I have all of the information he collected. If you put it together in just the right way, it will explain how to reverse the curse of The Bad Luck Chair. He wasn't able to. But *you* might be."

Addy didn't think so. If Lucky Odayo could not reverse the curse, then Bad-Luck-With-Many-Chairs-Not-Just-This-One Darby for sure could not, either.

"I need to go home," Addy said. She was getting that crying feeling again and didn't want tears to start dripping out right in the schoolyard. It was so cold they would probably freeze on her face. She walked away.

Katie called after her, but Addy kept moving. She wanted to get far, far away from The Chair.

Away from looking at it.

Away from sitting in it.

Especially away from talking about it with Katie O.

Addy just wanted to get home.

Never Sit Without Checking First

4

Home, Addy hummed as she turned the corner onto her street. She couldn't wait to step into her warm house. To be away from The Chair and all of the people who were staring at her because of it.

"Hi, Addy," voices called down. Addy looked up at *her* porch and saw two older kids sitting on the bench below *her* front window.

"Heard you sat in The Chair," the girl said.

"Wh-what?"

"Heard you sat in The Chair," she repeated.

"You did?" Addy asked.

The girl nodded. "Chair news travels fast. Especially to us," she added.

Addy now understood who these kids were. The girl

was Olivia Brown. The boy beside her was Ben Melman. Both of them were fifth-graders. And both had sat in The Chair.

"H-how come you're *here*?" Addy was still at the bottom of the porch steps.

Olivia shrugged. "Thought you might need some company."

Addy didn't want company. She wanted to be alone. Well, almost alone. She wanted to hang out with Herman. Cry to him about The Chair. But something deep inside was telling her to talk to Ben and Olivia. It was a strange, strong feeling. She climbed her steps, then got up the nerve to say, "Y-you guys w-want to come inside?"

Addy introduced her mom to Ben and Olivia. She knew that her mom would think the whole Chair thing was silly, just like Ms. Stern. So instead of telling her the *exact* truth, Addy said she was working on a school project with Olivia and Ben. Which, they all felt, wasn't totally a lie.

"For me, The Chair happened by accident," Olivia began as they sat at the kitchen table. "I was really late one morning because I couldn't find my favorite dance tights. I needed them because I was going to dance class straight from school. I came in after the final bell, so I had to run to my seat. Then I sat without checking."

You can never sit without checking first, Addy thought. That was school rule number one. "And then . . . what happened?" Addy asked softly. "Uh, are you . . . okay?"

"No," Olivia answered. "I'm not okay. I can't dance.

Not the way I used to, anyway." She closed her eyes, dropped her head, and added, "Let me put it to you this way: I don't exactly get the solos anymore."

It got quiet. A sad sort of quiet.

"The Chair happened to me because I was distracted," Ben said, breaking the silence. "It was a Friday morning," he went on. "The day of the MOT."

Addy nodded. She knew the MOT was the Math Olympian Test. Every second-grader took it, and the ones that did the best got to be official Brookside Math Olympians in third, fourth, and fifth grade. They got to go on special trips, like to a math museum and a *college* math class. And they got a special teacher once a week to teach them extra math stuff. It was a big honor.

"I was really nervous about it," Ben continued. "I'm good—well, I *was* good at math. But still, everyone knew how hard the MOT was. And I really, really wanted to be a Math Olympian. So when I walked into my classroom, I looked straight at the board for test instructions. That's where my teacher always wrote them." He paused, slumped back in his chair, and added, "While I was reading the board, I sat."

Addy sighed. "Sounds pretty bad."

"It was a disaster," Ben replied. "I failed the MOT. Didn't get to be an Olympian. And I'm still not as good in math as I used to be. Before The Chair."

Again, it was quiet. Again, it felt sad.

Addy knew it was her turn to talk.

She was shy at first. But as she went along, she could tell that Ben and Olivia really understood how she felt. The more they nodded and said things like, "Yeah, me too," the more it made her want to talk. She finished up by listing all the bad luck that had come her way. "I got into trouble with Ms. Stern," she said. "My drink leaked at lunch. Kids teased me about this embarrassing thing that happened last year. I got hit on the head with a ball during gym. I sneezed during silent reading time. *And*, to top off *the worst day I ever had*, Katie O. told me she had *secret* Chair information. So I met her after school, hoping she could help me. But all she did was make me feel worse."

"Worse? Why?" Olivia asked.

"Because there wasn't any *secret information*. There were just gory details about her brother. You know, all the bad stuff that happened to him after *he* sat in The Chair."

"Katie O.'s that fourth-grader who dresses sort of colorful, right?" Olivia asked.

"Uh-huh. She's in my class."

"Who's her brother?" Ben wondered.

"I don't know his name," Addy answered. "But I know people used to call him Lucky."

Olivia's eyes opened almost as wide as her mouth did.

Ben froze.

"What?" Addy asked.

Silence.

"What? T-tell me!" Addy pleaded.

"You don't know the *whole* Jonathan Odayo Chair

story," Olivia replied. She glanced at Ben, then looked back to Addy.

Addy shook her head. "I don't?" She was beginning to think that maybe she didn't want to. But that thought came about two seconds after Olivia began to tell it.

"Jon Odayo got hit harder by The Chair than anyone else, ever," she began. "Before The Chair he was like any other kid. Okay, maybe a little extra lucky, maybe a little extra brainy. But really, he was just a regular kid."

"And after?"

"After The Chair, he changed."

"How?" Addy asked.

"He got weird," Olivia answered. "Weird in a spooky kind of way."

Ben nodded an oversized nod.

"Spooky?" Addy brought her knees up and wrapped her arms around them.

"The way I heard the story, Jon stopped doing regular stuff," Olivia explained. "He didn't hang around after school."

"Didn't play ball in the park," Ben added.

"What *did* he do?" Addy wondered.

Olivia took a sip of juice. "That's the spooky part. I heard he turned his room into a science laboratory. No one is allowed up there. And except for school, he doesn't leave his lab."

"I heard that, too." Ben leaned forward and put his elbows on the table.

"*And,*" Olivia went on, "no one knows what kind of experiments he's doing there. He's all hush-hush about it."

Addy wondered if this science laboratory thing had anything to do with the *secret information* Katie had talked about. It was all starting to give her the creeps.

Brrrrring. The phone rang. Addy picked it up. "Hello?" she said.

"Hello," a voice said back. "Is this Addy?"

"Uh-huh. Wh-who's this?"

"It's Katie. Katie Odayo."

Addy felt her blood rush from her brain to her big toe. She figured her face must have looked funny, because Olivia stopped eating a pretzel and asked, "Who is it?"

Addy put her hand over the talk part of the phone and whispered, "It's K-Katie. Katie O."

Olivia and Ben sprang from their seats and ran to Addy. They both put their ears as close to the phone as they could.

"Are you still there?" Katie asked.

"Uh-huh."

"I'm sorry about what happened a little while ago," Katie said. "In the schoolyard. I didn't mean to make you feel so bad. But I really think you should look at the Chair stuff. Can you come over?" she asked.

"C-come over?" Addy repeated. Ben shook his head and

waved his hands. He scream-whispered, "No! Jon's Bad Luck Chair stuff must be really scary! Don't go over *there*!"

"Can you?" Katie asked again.

"Maybe you could bring his stuff to school," Addy tried.

"No," Katie answered.

"How come?" Addy asked.

"I just can't."

"Tell her you're busy," Olivia whispered. "Or you feel sick. Or you have too much homework. Anything!"

The last place on Earth that Addy wanted to go to was Katie's house. "Uh, Katie," she said, "I'm b-busy and I have a lot of homework and I feel sorta sick. Uh, bye." Addy hung up the phone and then took it off the hook so Katie couldn't call back.

Olivia and Ben burst into talk. "I thinks" and "maybes" and "what ifs" were popping out of their mouths. Finally they stopped and looked at Addy.

"You okay?" Olivia asked.

"No."

"I understand," Olivia said gently. "The first day in The Chair is hard."

"Yeah," Ben agreed. "I remember feeling *not* okay, too."

Ben and Olivia put their coats on. As they left, Olivia waved and called back, "See ya tomorrow."

Addy was in no rush for tomorrow.

Because tomorrow meant Day Two in The Chair.

Do Not Enter

5

Addy went to the bathroom to brush her teeth and get ready for Day Two. She flicked the light on but thought the room looked dark, like maybe one of the lightbulbs was out. And it was foggy, too, the way it might look after someone had taken a hot bath. But that didn't make any sense, so she slid the shower curtain back to see the tub.

The Chair! It was in the tub, sitting seat deep in water! Addy tried to scream, but no sound came out. She tried to run, but her legs wouldn't go. She was trapped in the bathroom with The Chair.

The Chair turned around in a complete circle, making the water swoosh and splash. Some spilled over the side of the tub and puddled on the green tile floor. Addy knew she was in her bathroom, but it looked different. Instead

of soap and toothpaste on the counter, she saw scientists' tools, like microscopes and test tubes. Underneath, the cabinet door was wide open. Instead of a hair dryer and extra toilet paper, Addy saw containers of ice cream. Green ice cream.

"I am going to get you, Addy!" The Chair roared.

"AHHHHHH!" Addy shot straight up. She thought she was in the bathroom, but she looked around and saw she was in her bedroom. In her bed.

"Is everything okay?" Addy's mom asked from the doorway. "You were screaming, sweetie. You must have had a nightmare."

Addy's heart was beating about a million times a minute. "Uh-huh, I did have a nightmare." *A Chair nightmare. A Chairmare!*

Her mom sat on the edge of her bed. "Want to talk about it?" she asked.

Addy described the nightmare to her mom. She told her about the giant chair that was going to attack her in the bathroom. Addy could hear how silly the whole thing sounded.

"Well, that's an *interesting* dream," her mom said, rubbing her back. "Why do you think you would dream something like that?"

Addy couldn't hold it in any longer. "Because there's a Bad Luck Chair in school, and it was by my desk yesterday, and Ms. Stern made me sit in it, and everyone was watching me, and—"

"A *bad luck chair?*"

"Uh-huh. Really."

"It sounds like a silly superstition, Addy," her mom replied. "Like black cats or not stepping on the cracks in the sidewalk. But I love black cats the most, and I always step on the cracks. Nothing bad happens."

Addy didn't know how to convince her mom that this was *not* just a silly superstition. It was real! So she skipped trying. "I asked Ms. Stern for a different chair, and she said she would ask the custodians."

"Good."

"But I still had to sit in it!"

"What's important is that you spoke up. I'm proud of you!" Addy's mom got up from the bed and added, "Would you like a glass of water, sweetie?"

"No, thanks."

"You ready to go back to sleep?" her mom asked, then yawned a loud, scales-on-a-piano yawn.

Addy nodded. There wasn't anything else to say.

After her mom went back to bed, Addy checked her clock. Four-thirty. Still three hours until she usually got up. She knew she should go back to sleep. But she was scared that if she did, she'd have another *Chairmare*. So she tried to stay awake. But even with her eyes open, all she did was think about The Chair. And the more she thought about it, the more afraid she became. *I have to figure out ways to not touch The Chair*, she thought to herself. *I need to find something thicker than the liner to put between me and The Chair. Something that would protect me even more from the Bad Luck.*

Addy decided that *that's* what she would do. She put on her robe and slippers, grabbed her flashlight, and snuck downstairs. She expected the dark to feel heavy and thick and full of doom. But compared to The Chair, the dark was a cinch.

She checked through closets, cabinets, and drawers. But it turned out that the perfect bad luck blocker was sitting right on the kitchen counter the whole time. The vegetable chopping board. It was the sure winner for three reasons:

1) It was clear, so Ms. Stern wouldn't be able to see it.
2) It was thick, so bad luck would have a hard time oozing through.
3) It had nonskid pads, so it would stay put.

Addy put it by her backpack and figured she'd ask if she could borrow it for her *project* in school. Her mom usually said yes when it came to school projects.

She crept back upstairs, feeling all clever and cool. Finding a vegetable chopping board in the dark may not have been as scary as standing in front of the whole class reading a book report. Still, doing *anything* that had *anything* to do with The Chair took guts. And for a kid who openly admitted to standing on the lowest rung of the gut ladder, Addy thought she did pretty well.

Hours later, in morning light, Addy put the clear vegetable chopping board on the seat of The Chair. It fit. And
it didn't shift or crinkle or make noise when she sat or got
up. It was perfect.

But her day was not. In art, Addy got stuck at the yellow
table. She spent forty-seven boring minutes mixing different shades of yellow for her monochromatic painting. She
wished she'd gotten blue.

On her pre-pre-pre spelling test, she got a 40. It didn't
count, but still, spelling was always easy for Addy. Now
she couldn't sound her way through simple words like *tis-
sue* and *shoelace* and *mustache*.

Plus, Katie O. kept bothering her. All day long Katie
urged her to *please, please* come to her house. "I'm positive my brother's Chair information can help you," she
said.

"I'm positive it can't," Addy replied. She did not understand how information that was still a secret could possibly
help her. And anyway, she dreaded the thought of getting
anywhere near the Bad Luck Laboratory.

Wednesday, Day Three, was worse. Even with the vegetable chopping board *and* the four pairs of underwear
Addy wore under her jeans for extra Chair protection,
bad luck kept on happening.

Her coat zipper got caught. She lost her homework. Her
pre-pre spelling test went just as badly as the pre-pre-pre.

By Wednesday afternoon, all that bad luck had wiped

Addy out. So when Katie O. handed her another triangle note, she didn't shake her head and say "No, thanks" the way she would have done just one day before. Instead, Addy read it:

> Dear Addy,
> I don't know why you don't believe me. I wouldn't make this up. I have important things to show you. They can help you figure out how to reverse the curse of The Bad Luck Chair. Please come to my house <u>today</u>!
>   Katie O.

Addy did not want to go. But she did believe Katie's note. At least the part about Katie not being the kind of kid who would make something up. So she finally said, "Okay, Katie, I'll come over to your house. But only if Sam can come with me." Addy looked at Sam to make sure that was okay with him. Sam blinked two times, then nodded.

"Deal," Katie replied. "Sam, too."

When they got to her house, Katie said, "This is my grandma. Grandma, this is Addy and Sam." Katie explained that her grandma stayed there in the afternoons until her mom and dad got home from work. Then she led

Addy and Sam up a tall flight of steps. "The Chair stuff is in my brother's room," she said, pointing to a door at the very end of the hall. It had a big wooden sign hanging on a chain that said, JON'S ROOM, then below that, DO NOT ENTER.

Addy wondered which was worse, sitting in The Chair or walking through That Door. The door that led to the secret laboratory and the *spooky* kid. "Katie," she said, "you sure this is okay?"

Katie didn't answer. She put her finger over her mouth and said, "*Shh.*"

Then she tapped on the door.

No answer.

She tapped again.

Still no answer.

Phew, Addy thought.

"The coast is clear. Let's go in," Katie whispered.

"In?" Addy asked. "In where?"

"In here!" Katie answered, pointing her thumb at Jon's door. "Today's Wednesday," she explained. "My brother's at Science Club." She checked her watch and added, "But we have to hurry. We need to be out before he gets home."

"J-Jon doesn't know that we're looking at his Chair stuff?" Addy whispered.

"Nope."

"Why not?"

"Because Jon doesn't know he still *has* his Chair stuff," Katie answered. "It's a long story," she went on. "I'll explain it all later." She put her hand over her heart and added, "I promise."

"But wh-what will happen if Jon catches us in his room?" Addy wondered.

Sam blinked two times. "Yeah, Katie. What will happen?" Sam repeated.

"You both *so* don't want to know." Katie checked over her shoulder, then put her hand on the doorknob. "Quick," she said. "Follow me."

Burp

6

Katie opened Jon's door and tiptoed in. The DO NOT ENTER sign swung and made a back-and-forth scratchy sound. The hairs on Addy's arms stood up.

"Come on!" Katie said.

Addy and Sam followed.

Katie closed the door behind them and left the light off. It was dark, but not so dark that Addy couldn't see Jon's room. It didn't look at all the way Addy had imagined it would. Olivia had said it was a science lab, but it was only a bedroom. An ordinary bedroom. There was a green rug on the floor and a plaid bedspread on the bed and a tall lamp on the nightstand.

But then Addy began to notice other things. Not mad scientist, scary things. Just things that seemed *less* ordinary to her. Like posters of the solar system on the walls. Like books on topics Addy couldn't pronounce on the shelves. Like a model of a human brain on the desk. Then Addy noticed one more thing. It was behind the brain, on the windowsill right above the desk. There, in a simple black frame, Addy saw an old, yellowed front page from *The West Elkwood Weekly*. The headline read: JONATHAN "LUCKY" ODAYO WINS FREE ICE CREAM FOR A YEAR! Addy figured that the picture under the headline must have been of Jon when he was in the fourth grade. He was in Ivan's Ice Cream World, holding a triple-decker cone with sprinkles. The framed article sat quietly on the sill. But in Addy's eyes and ears it shouted, *Look at me! This is who I was before The Chair!*

Katie opened Jon's closet door and pointed to its ceiling. "To get to the crawl space," Katie explained, "I have to climb through that."

Addy was pulled from her thoughts. She and Sam stuck their heads inside the closet to look. They saw a trapdoor just big enough for one person to climb through.

"Why would you need to get to the crawl space?" Addy asked.

"Because that's where I hid all of Jon's Chair stuff."

"Oh," was all Addy said. But inside her head, she was scream-thinking, *WHY, WHY, WHY ON EARTH WOULD YOU HIDE JON'S CHAIR STUFF IN A CRAWL SPACE OVER HIS ROOM? AND IF YOU DID DO THAT, WHY, WHY, WHY WOULD YOU WAIT UNTIL TODAY TO TAKE IT ALL DOWN?* She didn't ask, though. She knew it was part of the "long story" Katie promised to tell later.

"I'll climb up there to get everything," Katie said.

"Okay," Addy agreed, glad she didn't have to climb through a small door to get to a dark place to find scary stuff. "I'll stay right here so you can hand it down to me."

"And I'll be the lookout," Sam offered. He opened Jon's door a crack and leaned his ear against it.

Jon had stacks of bins and boxes on both sides of his closet. Katie was able to use them as steps, one side then the other, to work her way up to the top. When she was high enough, she pushed the door up and swung it open. Then she climbed in.

"Hope this doesn't take too long," Sam whispered to Addy, never taking his ear away from the door.

"I know, me too," Addy whispered back.

Addy and Sam could hear Katie moving around over their heads. It sounded like she was crawling on her hands and knees, which Addy thought made sense since she was in a *crawl* space. Finally Katie call-whispered from the open trapdoor, "Addy. You ready?"

"Ready," Addy answered. Katie lowered a shoe box to her. Addy stood on her toes and took it.

"There's more," Katie said. Addy put the box down and then stretched back up to take a big, black loose-leaf binder from Katie. She put that down, too, then took a thick book.

"Just one more thing," Katie said. "I have to go get it. Be right back."

Addy leaned on the frame of the closet door and looked at the pile in front of her. She wondered what was hidden in the shoe box, what was written in the binder, and what that particular book had to do with The Chair.

"Oh no!" Sam whisper-yelled. "Oh no—oh no—oh no! Addy! HE'S HOME!"

Addy felt panic blast through her body. She cupped her hands around her mouth and whisper-shouted to Katie, "HE'S HOME! HE'S HOME!"

Katie scrambled to the trapdoor. It sounded like an earthquake over their heads. "He's home?" Katie called back, her head hanging upside down.

"He's right at the bottom of the steps! He's coming up!" Sam closed the bedroom door.

Addy looked around the room. She couldn't find one good place to hide. There were books under the bed and books under the desk and books in the corner. "Katie," she called. "There's no place to hide. We have to come up!"

"Quick! Come up quick!" she answered.

Addy climbed the boxes the same way Katie had climbed them, only faster. When she was near the top, she grabbed the rim of the opening with both hands and flung herself in. She landed, then swung around on her knees and saw Sam right behind her. He threw himself in, too. As he hit the floor, Addy and Katie lifted the door and swung it shut. It closed about half a second before they heard Jon's bedroom door open.

Addy was shaking so hard she had to shut her mouth to keep her top teeth from hitting her bottom teeth and making noise. She opened her eyes extra wide to see as much as she could in the dusty blackness. It was a very big area, maybe as big as the whole upstairs of Katie's house. But the ceiling was low. She knew without trying that she couldn't stand. There were boxes and bags piled everywhere. And except for slivers of light that came through vents at both ends of the room, it was dark.

Addy and Sam and Katie sat next to one another, right by the closed door. They didn't move or speak. After a while, Addy's legs tingled and her eyes stung. She shifted her weight to try to get more comfortable.

"Don't worry," Katie said in a very quiet whisper. "If we stay just like this, over his closet, he'll never know we're here."

Addy gasped.

Katie and Sam shushed her.

"The closet!" Addy whispered. "I left all the Chair stuff you handed me down in the closet!"

"*For real?*" Sam asked.

"Uh-huh." Addy's eyes had adjusted to the dark. She saw Sam blink.

"Was it totally *in* the closet?" Katie asked. "Or was it sticking *out?*"

Addy tried to picture the spot where she had left the pile. But she just couldn't see it in her mind. "I don't r-remember exactly."

They were quiet again. But this time Addy wasn't thinking about her dry throat or stiff legs. All she could think about was *where* that pile was. "I think if I get on my stomach and put my head right by this door, I can open it a tiny bit and peek," she said.

Katie agreed. "Good idea."

"We have to be careful the floor doesn't creak," Sam added. "We can't make *any* noise."

Slowly, Addy, Sam, and Katie all got onto their stomachs. When everyone was ready, Addy gently lifted the door and wedged it open with her hand. Light and air streamed in.

Addy saw that the pile of Chair stuff was *inside* Jon's closet. *Good*, she thought. But she could also see that the closet door was open. She wasn't sure where Jon was, but she could hear him moving around his room. If he moved toward his closet, he could easily see the stuff.

"Grandma," he called.

Addy was so startled she almost dropped the door.

"Grams," Jon called again, "have you seen my calculator? I have a lot of math homework, and I don't remember where I left it."

"It's here, on the kitchen desk," his grandma called back up.

Then everything was quiet. Addy figured that Jon must have gone downstairs.

"You think we have time to get out of here?" Sam asked Katie.

"Yup! I think so!" Katie answered.

Addy swung the door open. Katie took the last of the Chair stuff, which was one more book, handed it to Sam, and said, "Toss this to me when I'm out." Then she turned around and with her back to the door added, "Watch how I get down. It's like this." She stood over the opening, then grabbed onto small handles on both sides.

Addy hadn't noticed they were there.

Then Katie dropped one leg down and said, "This side is better to start." Her left leg found the highest bin. "Then just go down the way you came up. See?" She leaned back and forth, finding a box or bin with one foot, then the other, until her feet were firmly on the floor.

"What are you doing in my closet?" Jon said.

"Huh?" Katie answered.

Addy covered her mouth with both hands. Sam suddenly looked blurry through the tears in her eyes.

"What are you doing here?" Jon asked again. He sounded mad.

Katie shut the closet door. The crawl space got dark.

"Looking for my, er, my flashlight," Katie answered. "I thought you might have put it away in your closet."

It was harder to hear what they were saying with the closet door shut. Addy had to really concentrate.

"Remember? You borrowed it last week," Katie went on.

"It's right in front of you. On my desk," Jon replied. "Do you need stronger glasses or something?"

"Oh. Thanks. I didn't see it."

Then Addy heard nothing. She and Sam sat perfectly still, wondering what was going on. Wondering where Katie was. Wondering if they would ever get out of the crawl space alive.

"Sam," Addy whispered. Her eyes had adjusted to the dim light again and she could sort of see him. Sam shook his head and waved his hands. *"No noise,"* he whispered back.

They waited and waited. Addy wished it was a regular Wednesday afternoon. That was her favorite part of the week, when she and Sam had their Word Nerd meetings. Sometimes they worked on word searches. Other times crosswords. One time they made Word Nerd membership cards, with photos and signatures. Addy was proud of her card and carried it with her everywhere. The last couple of meetings had been the best, though. They had decided to write their own word puzzle book. They were almost done, and it was coming out great.

"Sam," she whispered, "don't you wish we were—"

"Shhh!" he said. "No noise!"

It was hard to just sit there and wait. Addy began to imagine all the ways they could get caught. For one, she had given her mom Katie's address and phone number when they called from the school office. Her mom could call any second to check on when she needed a ride home. For another, Katie's grandma could tell them to all come down for a snack. Or, even more horrifying, Jon could go into his closet for something. Or . . .

BURP!

OR SAM COULD BURP!

For someone who was big on *no noise*, Addy thought Sam burped pretty noisily.

They froze. There was nothing they could do and no place they could go. Addy just waited to get caught. *Any minute now*, she thought. *Any second now, Jon's going to swing that door open and look for where that burp came from.* And then, well, then she wasn't sure what. But she was sure it would not be good. She closed her eyes and waited, like she was in the doctor's office and was about to get a shot.

"Jon?" Katie called. "Jon?"

Addy opened her eyes. Katie was back in Jon's room.

"What?" Jon said. His voice sounded loud, like he was right outside the closet door.

"Something's wrong with the toaster oven," Katie answered. "Grandma can't get it to work."

"So."

"So could you try to fix it?"

"I have a lot of math homework," Jon answered.

"But Grams wants to warm something up."

"Right now?"

"Yup. Right now."

Everything got quiet.

"You think he's still in the room?" Addy asked Sam.

"I'm not sure," Sam answered.

Then, without any warning, the closet door swung open!

Addy screamed a silent scream. She saw Sam jump back, away from the trapdoor.

"Addy! Sam!" Katie called.

"Katie! I thought you were Jon!" Addy whispered back.

"Me too!" Sam said.

"Jon's downstairs trying to fix the toaster oven. I un-plugged it," Katie explained. "Quick, get out. I gotta get back down there to stall him. Meet me in my room." Katie ran off.

Addy grabbed the handles and climbed out just like Katie had. It was easy. Sam dropped the book down to her, came out, then pulled the trapdoor shut. Together they swooped the chair stuff up and tore out of Jon's room. They ran down the hall into the only open door. Addy was sure it was Katie's room because it was so colorful.

Seconds later, Katie flew into her room, too.

"Holy Ravioli," Sam said, dropping to the carpet.

"Holy *Moly* Ravioli," Addy replied, falling right beside him.

Katie closed the door and leaned her back against it. "*Way* Holy Moly Ravioli," she added. Then she slid down, too.

Error

7

Addy, Sam, and Katie looked like three stuffed animals at a tea party. Three shook-up, flipped-out stuffed animals. They sat on Katie's yellow shag rug and stared at one another.

Until it happened again. Sam burped. And then, like three bubblegum bubbles blown too big, Addy and Sam and Katie popped, bursting into laughter. Not a *ha-ha, that was so funny* kind of laughter. Addy and Sam and Katie laughed a crazy, out-of-control, tears in your eyes, you-can't-stop-even-though-you-really-want-to, it hurts kind of laughter. And when they finally calmed down and stopped, they felt better.

"I guess sometimes scary things are funny after they happen," Addy said.

"I guess sometimes scary things make me burp," Sam added.

Katie agreed with both of them.

"Do you want to hear the *whole story* now?" Katie asked. She was still wiping laughter tears from her eyes.

"Uh-huh," Addy answered. "We really do."

"Okay," Katie said. "I'll tell you *everything*. But I have to talk really low so *no one* hears." She tipped her head in the direction of Jon's room. Addy and Sam moved closer to Katie on the rug.

"I'm kind of happy to finally be telling you this," Katie began. "It was hard *not* to talk about it for so long." She crossed her legs and took a deep breath.

Addy could see how hard this was for Katie.

"You already know that Jon sat in The Chair when he was in fourth grade," she said. "And you already know that he was really lucky before The Chair, and after, er, not so lucky."

"Yuh-huh," Sam replied.

"But what you don't know is that Jon's like a genius when it comes to science," Katie explained. "So he decided to look at The Chair like it was a science experiment. He wanted to figure it out so he could fix it. And turn his bad luck back to good."

"Wow. What happened?" Addy asked.

"At first, it went really well," Katie said. "He did a lot of research and took a lot of notes and spoke with a bunch of people. He was pretty sure he was going to figure it out."

"And then?" Sam wondered.

"Then he got stuck. Because just when he thought he had it all figured out, he figured out one more important thing." Katie stretched her legs out in front of her. "He figured out that *he* would never be able to reverse the curse."

"Never?" Addy asked. "So The Chair will always be The Chair? And the curse can *never* be reversed?"

"The curse *can* be reversed," Katie answered. "But not by Jon."

Sam leaned forward and put his elbows on his knees. "I don't get it, Katie. By who, then?"

"He didn't know. But he knew it was only *one* person. And he knew it wasn't him." Katie shook her head. "He was so frustrated. Plus, right around the same time, my mom and dad were all worried about him. They thought he was spending too much time in his room. They didn't understand why he wasn't hanging out with his friends anymore. And then the teacher called to say that his grades were going down."

"Sounds like it was a bad time for him," Addy said.

"It was a terrible time," Katie replied. "So when Jon realized that, after all the work he put into it, he would never be able to reverse the curse, he gave up. He packed all of his Chair stuff into a garbage bag and threw it out! And he never said another word about it."

Addy and Sam sat still and listened, like they were watching a movie and didn't want to miss one thing.

"I couldn't believe it," Katie continued. "I mean, he worked so hard. And he got so close." She stood up and walked around in a circle.

Addy could see how upset she was. "So you saved the stuff for him?" she asked.

"Yup," Katie answered. She sat back down on the rug. "That night, after everyone went to sleep, I snuck downstairs and pulled all of his Chair stuff out of the garbage can in the garage. For a while, I hid it under my bed. But I knew that if my mom found it, I'd be in big trouble. So one day when my dad was putting old clothes up in the crawl space, I snuck Jon's Chair stuff up there, too. And I promised myself I wouldn't bring it back down until I was sure that I needed it." She paused, then looked at Addy. "I was hoping that one day I would need it to finish the project for him. I was hoping I would find the person, the one person, who can reverse the curse."

"You think Addy's that person?" Sam asked.

"Maybe," Katie answered. "I mean, she's the first fourth-grader to sit in it since Jon. And I remember Jon saying he was pretty sure that the person would be in fourth grade, just like he was."

"Really?" Addy asked.

"Yup. And, it *is* sort of a weird coincidence that we're in the same class when you got stuck with The Chair, right?" Katie asked.

"It is." Addy nodded.

"Actually," Katie continued, "we don't have to wonder about it. There's a way to find out."

"There is?" Addy asked.

Katie smiled. "Yup. See, Jon didn't mind me hanging around his room while all this was going on," she explained. "He even used to tell me everything he was doing. He probably figured that I was too young to really understand. But I understood a lot of it. And I know he put a bunch of questions on the computer. He even tried it out on me once, so I know how it works. He programmed the computer to organize and decode the answers. The person who answers all of the questions the right way," Katie explained, "is the one. The one person who can reverse the curse of The Bad Luck Chair. And break the spell for anyone who ever sat in it."

"Wowville," Addy said.

"For real, wowville," Sam agreed.

"So, do you want to try to answer the questions?" Katie asked.

"Uh, I—I guess so," Addy answered. "Are they tricky?"

"Nope, not at all," Katie assured her.

"Just think of it as a puzzle, Addy," Sam suggested, "and take it one question at a time."

"O-okay."

Katie got up and made sure that all of the Chair stuff was covered by other things in her closet. Then the three of them went down to the den. It was in the back of the house, behind the kitchen. Katie's grandma was at the kitchen table, reading the newspaper and drinking a cup of coffee. She waved as they passed her. "You hungry?" she asked.

"Nah," Katie answered.

Addy was starving, but she didn't say anything.

Katie sat at the desk in the den and turned the computer on. Five names popped up on the screen: Rob, Lori, Jon, Katie, and Grams. Katie double-clicked on Jon's name.

"Isn't this, like, illegal?" Sam asked.

"Er, I'm not sure," Katie answered.

Please enter password came up on the screen.

Addy and Sam sat in folding chairs right next to Katie.

"You know his password?" Addy whispered.

Katie shook her head. "No," she answered. "But I was hoping we could figure it out." Then she typed in the word *science* and pressed ENTER. It was invalid. She tried *solar-system*. Invalid. *Algebra*. Invalid. *Earth*. Invalid. *Brain*. Invalid.

"Is there a girl he likes?" Addy asked. Then she giggled.

Samantha. Invalid.

Brooke. Invalid.

MrsHopson. Invalid.

"He likes a *teacher*?" Sam asked.

"It's his science teacher," Katie explained.

"How about sports teams?" Sam tried.

Elks. Invalid.

Cougars. Invalid.

Katie put her hands in her lap and looked at Addy. "I thought this would be easy," she said. "I didn't think he'd have such a tough password."

Addy closed her eyes and thought hard. She held the ladybug charm on her necklace and slid it back and forth on its chain. Over and over she repeated, "Jon's password, Jon's password." And then it came to her. "I got it," she said. "I think I know what his password is."

Sam and Katie looked at her.

"Try *Lucky*," she said.

"*Lucky*?" Katie repeated. "He wouldn't use *Lucky* as a password. I told you that was a long time ago, Addy. He doesn't talk about that anymore."

"Just try it, okay?" Addy asked.

Katie typed L-U-C-K-Y.

And up popped the words: *Welcome, Jon.*

Addy thought she saw Katie wipe away a quick tear.

Katie read through Jon's files. She found one called *Bad Luck Chair* and double-clicked it. "Yup, this is it," she said. "You ready?"

"Ready," Addy answered.

Katie read question one aloud from the screen. "How old are you?"

"Nine, almost ten."

"But you're still nine, right?" Katie asked.

"Yup. My birthday's not until May," Addy answered. And as she did, she thought about how much fun it would be to have a small party this year and invite Sam *and* Katie.

Katie typed 9 into the computer. The words CORRECT
- - PLEASE CONTINUE appeared.

"Okay," Katie said. "Good. Number two. What grade
are you in?"

"You know what grade I'm in!" Addy answered.

"I know. But let's do this right. Like Jon would, okay?"

"Okay, okay. I'm in fourth grade," Addy answered.

- - - - CORRECT - - PLEASE CONTINUE - - - -

"What room number were you in when you sat in The
Chair?"

"Thirty-six."

- - - - CORRECT - - PLEASE CONTINUE - - - -

"What was the outside air temperature when you sat
in it?"

"I'm not sure," Addy answered. "It was about the same
as it is today. What's today's temperature?"

Katie got up from the chair and looked at the thermom-
eter suctioned to the outside of the den window. "It's
thirty degrees."

"Okay, about thirty degrees then," Addy said. She bit
her lip and waited.

- - - - CORRECT - - PLEASE CONTINUE - - - -

"What color is your hair?"

"You can't see what color her hair is?" Sam asked.

"Of course I can see. But I want to do this the right way.
Just answer the questions, Addy, okay?"

"Fine. Brown."

- - - - CORRECT - - PLEASE CONTINUE - - - -

"Eye color?"

"Brown."

- - - - CORRECT - - PLEASE CONTINUE - - - -

"Boy or girl?"

"GIRL!"

- - - - CORRECT - - PLEASE CONTINUE - - - -

"First letter of your last name?"

"*D*, for Darby."

- - - - CORRECT - - PLEASE CONTINUE - - - -

"The next question is the last," Katie said. "Everyone, cross your fingers. If this answer is correct, Addy is the

person, the *only* person, who can reverse the curse." She shook her hands out. "Addy, you ready?"

"I'm in Readyville."

"It's an easy one," Katie said. "Tell me the *first* letter of your *first* name."

"*A!*" Sam yelled.

Katie typed A into the computer.

- - - - - - - - - - - ERROR - - - - - - - - - - - -

"Wait," Katie said. "Maybe I pressed the wrong letter." She pressed the A key again.

- - - - - - - - - - - ERROR - - - - - - - - - - - -

A

- - - - - - - - - - - ERROR - - - - - - - - - - - -

A

- - - - - - - - - - - ERROR - - - - - - - - - - - -

"Oh no!" Katie cried out. "This is terrible, Addy. After all that, you're not *the one*. Your first name starts with an *A!*"

The Secret

8

"I have a secret," Addy said. "A big one." She got up from the folding chair and sat down on the big, cushy couch. She felt very small. No one even heard her.

Katie kept typing the letter *A* into the computer. Sam kept trying to help. "Put in a lowercase *a*," he said. When that didn't work, he told Katie, "Maybe you have to write her whole name, not just the first letter." But no matter what Katie did, ERROR kept popping up on the screen.

"I have a secret," Addy said again, this time louder. Again Sam and Katie didn't pay any attention. They were still too busy trying to un-error the error.

"MY FIRST NAME DOESN'T START WITH THE LETTER *A*!" Addy shouted.

They turned to her.

"Yes, it does," Sam said. He blinked two times. Then, in

a calm and gentle voice, he added, "Addy, your name starts with the letter *A*. Aah"—he sounded it out for her— "Aah-dee. See. It starts with an *A* sound. Aah."

Addy rolled her eyes as far back into her head as they would go. "Sam. I know the first letter of my first name. It's not *A*!"

"Maybe this whole Chair thing is making you feel, um, *confused*." Blink. Blink.

"No, I'm not confused."

"Yes, Aah-dee. You are confused."

Addy shook her head. "I know what letter my name starts with. It's not *A* because . . . because my name isn't really Addy."

"Addy, cut it out!" Sam warned. "You're acting funny and I'm getting all porcupine!" He rubbed the goose bumps that popped out on his arms. Then he blinked again.

Addy looked around. She saw Katie by the desk. She had a kind, caring look on her face. Like she had just found a hurt animal and she wanted to try to help it. And Addy saw Sam, her very best friend. Her fellow Word Nerd Club member. Sam looked scared.

"My first name isn't really Addison," she explained. "Addison is my middle name, but it's the one I go by."

"How come?" Katie asked. She sat down on the couch next to Addy.

"Because my first name is too embarrassing."

"Too embarrassing?"

"Uh-huh. It's bad. My mom named me after her favorite flower."

"How do the teachers know to call you Addison?" Katie wondered. "Isn't your real name on the class list the first day of school?"

"The nice lady in the office, Mrs. Hibbard, changed it for me," Addy explained. "At kindergarten orientation, Mrs. Hibbard saw me covering my name tag and asked me why. I told her because I didn't want kids to laugh at my name. She read my tag and asked, 'Do they laugh at you?' I said that sometimes they did, in pre-K. I asked her if she would put Addy on my name tag, because everyone at home called me that anyway."

"But what about on the attendance list?" Katie asked. "Did Mrs. Hibbard change it there, too?"

Addy nodded. "That morning, she changed it on my name tag. Later, she checked with my mom. My mom said it was okay to change it on the attendance list, too, since even *she* called me Addy."

Sam still sat on the folding chair by the desk. He still looked porcupine. And hurt. "Addy, or whatever your name is, I can't believe you never told me this," he said. "I thought we were best friends. You know tons of *my* secrets. I don't even know your name!"

"Don't be mad, Sam." She explained that Addy started as a nickname when she was very little, and it just stuck. That she used Addy for so long, it sort of became her real name. That she wasn't hiding her name from him, she just wasn't thinking about it. "Until now," she said. "When the computer said 'Error.' So please, Sam. Please don't be mad."

Sam crossed his arms and asked, "What's your name? Your *real* name."

"You're mad at me, aren't you?"

Sam looked away.

Addy felt sad. And lost. And all alone in a bubble of bad luck.

Your best friend being mad at you was the worst, worst luck of all. Worse, even, than having to tell people your embarrassing first name.

"Okay," Addy said softly. "I give up. I'll tell."

"Wait," Katie said. "That's not fair. If you have to tell a big secret, I should have to also."

"No, really, you don't have to do that."

"I *do*," Katie insisted. "It's not right for me to know something about you without you knowing something about me."

"That's really nice of you," Addy said.

Katie smiled, then looked like she was deciding what secret she would tell. "Okay," she began in a whisper. "Don't tell anyone." She looked at Sam and Addy. "Last year, on a class trip, I, er, wet my pants."

"*You made in your pants?*" Addy whispered back.

"Kind of. We were on the bus, coming home. I was sitting in the backseat when someone said something really funny. So I started to laugh, and while I was laughing, the bus hit a bump. And you know how in the backseat the bumps are really bumpy?"

"I know!" Sam said. "I love the backseat on a bus! It's the best!"

"Me, too! Anyway, I'm laughing really hard and then I bounce about ten feet in the air from this sudden bump. And then, I don't know, it just . . . happened."

Addy giggled. "It's sort of funny," she said.

Katie smiled. "Yeah, it is." Then she finished by saying, "It wasn't that bad. It was only a little and I was wearing dark pants, so no one knew."

"My turn," Sam called out.

"No, you don't have to tell a secret," Katie said.

"I want to," he replied. "It'll feel even that way. I just have to think of a good one."

Addy looked at Sam and said, "Tell her the one about the soup."

Sam smiled. "That's a good one. But Katie, if you ever meet anyone in my family, you can't tell." Katie nodded, and Sam pulled his chair closer to the couch.

"I was at my cousin's wedding," Sam began. "And they served soup. It tasted great, so I took a big mouthful. That exact second, my sister went up to the microphone and sang a *love song* to the bride and groom. It was for supreme real, *ewww*. I didn't want to laugh because my parents would've gotten mad. But it was hard to hold the laugh in. I don't know how it happened, but all of a sudden soup started coming out of my nose. And while the soup was coming out, the bride passed by me to go hug my sister. My *nose-soup* spilled all over her left shoe!"

"No way!" Katie called out.

"For real, it did! I thought I was in big trouble. I thought the bride was going to whip that shoe off her foot and hit me over the head with it. Or maybe my dad would make me go sit in the car. But no one saw. Not *one* person at the whole wedding saw the green goo flow from my nostrils onto the bride's white shoe!"

Katie and Addy were laughing so hard they slipped off the front of the couch.

Then, from her spot on the floor, Addy said that she was ready. "But you have to promise never to tell anyone. Ever. Okay? Because I really don't like it when people laugh at me. I'm super-sensitive that way. Especially after, ya know, the thing last year."

"I understand," Katie said. "I don't like being laughed at, either."

"Really?" Addy asked. "Because you seem really confident to me. Quiet, but confident. I mean, you always wear fun, bright clothes. And you don't seem to care what people think."

"I care," Katie answered. "But I don't think people really understand me." She shrugged, then went on. "I want to be a fashion designer when I grow up. So I like to dress in all different kinds of things. Put fun stuff together and try it out. Kids just think I'm weird."

"I think you're cool," Addy replied. "Really. I always have. I wish I had the guts to dress like you."

"Then why don't you?" Katie asked.

"I don't know. I just couldn't," Addy answered. "Everyone would look at me."

"You could start with small things," Katie suggested. "Like, if you wanted to, you could wear fun shoelaces. I have a bunch of colors that you could borrow."

Addy shrugged. "I'll think about it." Then she cupped her hands around her mouth, and in a teeny-tiny whisper, told Sam and then Katie her real name.

Katie went back to the desk and entered the first letter of Addy's real first name into the computer: P.

- - - - CORRECT - - - -

- - - - INFORMATION COMPLETE - - - -

- - - - INDIVIDUAL LOCATED - - - -

"*P!*" Katie called to Addy. "You're *the one*! You're *the one* who can reverse the curse!"

"Wah-hoo!" Addy cheered. She held her hands high in a victory V over her head. Then she and Sam double high-fived.

"You're not still mad, are you, Sam?" she asked.

"No," Sam answered.

Addy felt like her luck was changing already.

"I am in Happyville!" Addy announced. She plopped down in her spot, on the folding chair next to Katie. "Let's reverse the curse!" she said. "What do I do, Katie? Chant some words? Boil some water? Click my heels?"

Katie turned her chair to Addy. "Actually," she replied, "I think it's more complicated than that. We have to go back upstairs and start going through all of Jon's Chair stuff."

"Okay," Addy said. "Then let's go up. But," she added, then suddenly felt shy again. Still, she said it anyway. "But, I'm starving, Katie. Can we have a snack first?"

After two donuts and a tall glass of milk each, Addy, Sam, and Katie went back up to Katie's room. Katie shut her door and got all of Jon's Chair stuff out of her closet. She put it on her yellow rug, and they sat down around it.

"The black binder has all of Jon's notes," Katie began. "Most of it I don't understand, and I don't think it matters. It's a lot of math calculations and charts and things. I saved it just in case. The books," she went on, "were the books Jon used the most. I thought we might need them." Then she opened the shoe box. "I don't know why these things are important, but I know that they are." First, Katie took out a stack of photos, held together with a rubber band. Addy slipped the rubber band off. "They're all of the schoolyard," she said, flipping through, one by one.

"Look," Sam said. He took the photos and set them down on the rug, next to one another. "If you line them up like this, it looks like one big picture. They all connect."

Addy could see what Sam meant. It was as if Jon picked a spot and just kept taking pictures while he turned around in place.

"Is Jon very tall?" Addy asked Katie.

"Nope. Why?" Katie asked back.

"I don't know. It just seems like the pictures were taken by a tall person," Addy answered.

Next, Katie took out a big, square battery, a roll of coated wire, and a piece of thin paper.

"What's all this for?" Addy asked.

"I don't know," Katie answered. "But I know they go together, because Jon kept them all in one small box."

Last, Katie took a sealed envelope from the box and handed it to Addy. "What's in this envelope is the *most important thing*," she said.

"Should I open it?" Addy asked.

"Yup."

Sam blinked.

Addy carefully tore the top open. Inside was a single sheet of paper, folded in thirds. She took it out and unfolded just the top section. It read:

HOW TO REVERSE THE CURSE OF THE BAD LUCK CHAIR

"Wow!" Addy said. Her heart raced. She held that piece of paper like it was a speedy dog off its leash. Like if she let go for just a second, that paper dog would be gone and she could never run fast enough to catch up with it.

That one piece of paper could fix everything.

"But here's the problem," Katie said. "Only *you* can understand the instructions. Jon couldn't. He figured out what they *were*. But he couldn't figure out what they *meant*."

"How could that be?" Addy asked. "He wrote them!"

"What he wrote is a list. He worked really hard and did a lot of research to write it," Katie explained. "To *you*, it's instructions. To everyone else, it's just a list."

Addy felt half and half, like a black-and-white cookie from the bakery. The vanilla side felt like there was no way she would be able to pull this off. She was just a quiet fourth-grader who had one, *maybe two* friends, and was proud to be a member of The Word Nerd Club. She was no pirate looking for an adventure. But the other part, the chocolate part, felt special. Maybe she really was *the one*. Maybe she would be able to understand the instructions that no one else could. And maybe, maybe she'd be able to follow them and reverse the curse of The Bad Luck Chair.

"You ready to read the instructions?" Katie asked.

"I always liked chocolate," Addy answered.

"What?"

"Nothing. I'm ready."

With Sam looking over one shoulder and Katie looking over the other, Addy unfolded the rest of the paper. She read Jon's typed instructions:

HOW TO REVERSE THE CURSE OF THE BAD LUCK CHAIR

1. Remove the correct piece.
2. Change its direction to make it an opposite.
3. Keep it close.
4. At time of birth, birthday backwards, set Chair in sight of water and sit.
5. Surround it by 42 and spin, by way of hand—2 times for each plus 1 time reversed to equal 13.
6. Count up to the number between, find the right rhyme, and scream!

"Does it make sense to you?" Katie asked.

"Do you *get* it?" Sam asked.

They were making Addy nervous.

She read through Jon's instructions a second time. And a third. Then she put the sheet of paper down on Katie's rug and answered both of them with one short, disappointing word. "No."

The Correct Piece

9

"No?" Katie asked.

"No as in *no know*?" Sam asked.

"No, as in I don't have a clue," Addy answered. "No, as in *not even one* of the things on that list means anything to me. No, as in I don't think I'm really *the one* because I don't think I am ever going to be able to reverse the curse of The Bad Luck Chair!" She got up and looked out the window. She had *so* wanted to understand the instructions. Had *so* thought that she'd be able to. She was embarrassed for feeling that way.

No one said anything for a long time. Finally, Sam spoke. "I think you can do it, Addy. I mean it. I know those instructions are confusing. But they remind me of word puzzles. And you're really good at them."

Addy sat back down and listened.

"Like remember the time we were working on that crazy cryptoquote at a Word Nerd meeting? Remember? We were working on it all afternoon and it was really hard and I gave up. But you kept working on it. And then all of a sudden, you figured it out!"

Addy nodded. She remembered how hard that cryptoquote was.

"And what about the time we had that tall substitute teacher," Sam continued. "Mr. Jalo-something? He brought in the game with the letter cubes. You shook the cubes and spilled them out of the cup. And then you found about a million words that *all* had *all* of those letters in them. You won the game!"

Addy remembered that, too. It was the only time this whole school year when she had done something that called attention to herself. Until now.

"*I* remember that," Katie said. She looked at Addy and added, "I wanted to go over to you and tell you how amazing I thought you were."

"Really?"

"Yup. Really."

Addy took the paper. "Do you honestly think I can pull this off, Sam?" she asked.

Sam nodded. "For supreme real, I honestly think you can pull this off," he answered. "But you have to be brave about it. You have to really try."

Addy looked at the list again. "One," she read. "Remove the correct piece. *Remove the correct piece*," she repeated softly.

Sam and Katie sat very still.

Addy thought very hard. She slid her necklace back and forth, back and forth.

"Nothing," she said. "Nothing's happening."

"Try not to force it," Katie said.

"Yeah, just take it easy," Sam agreed.

Addy thought some more. She rubbed small circles over her eyes. "Nothing," she said again. "And I know why."

"Why?" Sam asked.

"I can't figure anything out because The Chair isn't letting me," Addy explained. "The Chair attacks the thing a person does best, the thing that's most special about them. I was thinking about it since Monday, when I talked to Olivia and Ben," she went on. "Olivia can't dance anymore. Ben can't do math." She looked at Katie and added softly, "Jon used to be lucky and now, ya know . . ."

"I know."

"So you think The Chair took away your supreme talent with letters and words?" Sam asked.

Addy shrugged. "Maybe. I mean, I failed the pre-pre-pre and the pre-pre spelling tests this week. I know spelling isn't the same thing as word puzzles. But they both have to do with letters. And I'm a good speller."

Katie was quiet for a little while. Then she said, "I remember that after Jon sat in The Chair, his luck went away. But it didn't happen all at once," she added. "It went away a little at a time."

"So you're saying I might still have some word ability left in me?"

"Yup. I bet you do," Katie answered. "You're probably not as good as you were. But you're also probably not as bad as you're going to be."

What Katie said made Addy antsy. She felt like she was in a race with The Chair. She had to understand the instructions before The Chair swallowed up *all* of her word skills. She held the paper in front of her and read instruction number one again. *Remove the correct piece.* She closed her eyes and concentrated. "Maybe it means to take a piece off of The Chair?" she asked out loud. "But which piece is the *correct* piece? Hmmm. To *correct* would mean to fix or repair," she said. "Everyone who sat in The Chair wants to be repaired. We all want to go back to being the way we were before."

"Keep going," Sam said. "You're doing great, Addy."

"On Monday, when Olivia Brown and Ben Melman came to my house, I wasn't in the mood to talk about The Chair. But my gut feeling was to talk to them anyway. And my gut feeling again, right now, is that they have something to do with this. It's about reversing the curse for *everyone*, right?"

"Right," Katie answered. "But when you say *everyone*, who do you mean?"

"The Chair's been around for a long time," Sam added. "There have been a lot of sitters. We don't even know all of them."

"Well," Addy said, "this whole thing began with Jon doing the research. And maybe, hopefully, it will end with me following his instructions. So I would say all of the sitters between Jon and me have something to do with the reverse."

Katie leaned toward her nightstand and opened the drawer in it. She pulled out a pad and pencil. "Okay," she said. "Let's figure out who those sitters are."

Addy closed her hand and then counted on her fingers, thumb first. "Right after Jon there was Ben Melman," she said.

Katie wrote his name down.

Addy opened her pointer finger. "Then Olivia Brown," she said.

Katie added Olivia to the list.

"Then last year two kids sat in it. Remember?" Sam added.

"Uh-huh, that's right," Addy agreed. "They were both second-graders. First, Lucy Pollick, and then . . . uh, Troy Michaels." All of her fingers were open now except for her pinky.

"And then . . . *you* sat in it, Addy," Sam said.

Addy looked at her hand. "So that means there were four sitters between Jon and me."

"Yup," Katie replied, then handed Addy the list.

Addy reached for it and said, "I'm not really sure what these four sitters . . ." She stopped talking.

"What?" Sam asked. "You okay, Addy? Is something wrong?"

Addy turned the list so Sam and Katie could read it. "Look!" she said. "The *correct piece* is right in front of us! I can't believe it took me this long to figure it out. It's so simple! Look!" She put the pad down on the rug and they both leaned over it to see.

"Where?" Sam asked.

"Show me!" Katie called out.

Addy pointed to the first initial of each sitter's name.

Ben Melman
Olivia Brown
Lucy Pollick
Troy Michaels

"B-O-L-T," she said. "Bolt! That's the correct piece!"

"BOLT!" they all screamed. They sprang up and started jumping around in a circle. "A bolt," they sang. "A B-O-L-T bolt!"

"See, Addy?" Sam said. "You really are *the one*! You were able to figure that out!"

"All I have to do is remove a bolt from The Bad Luck Chair," Addy replied in a high, happy voice.

She stopped jumping. "Wait a minute," she said. "How am I supposed to get a *bolt* off of The Chair?"

Sam and Katie were quiet.

"Really, how?" she asked again.

"I don't know," Katie answered. "Maybe we should brainstorm."

Sam laughed.

"What's so funny?" Katie asked.

"It's just that I've always pictured a brainstorm to look like a blizzard with brains blowing all over the place," Sam answered.

"*Ewww!*" Katie giggled. "That's so yuck!"

Addy, Sam, and Katie sat back down on the rug. Addy began the brainstorm by saying, "I definitely don't want to *touch* The Chair. So I don't know how I can take something off of it." She held her hands out, fingers up.

"I don't think you should touch it, either," Sam agreed. "That would be too scary." He thought for a minute and then added, "How about you wear gloves?"

"But won't it be hard for her to get a small bolt off of The Chair if she's wearing winter gloves?" Katie asked. "They're so thick and stiff."

Addy nodded. "How about those tight rubber gloves?" she asked. "The kind dentists wear so your spit doesn't drip all over them. I think if I were wearing a pair of those, my fingers would still be able to move around."

"I have a pair you can use," Katie said. "Last summer

in camp we tie-dyed shirts. The counselor gave out gloves so we didn't tie-dye our hands. After we finished, we were supposed to throw the gloves out. But I really liked how mine turned a see-through red. So I took them home."

In no time at all, Addy, Sam, and Katie figured out a way to take a bolt off of The Chair. Katie gave Addy a new sheet of paper, a pencil, and an orange clipboard.

Addy wrote down everything she needed to do. She tried to keep it organized and neat. It was the first real plan she ever wrote. She wanted it to look official.

Reverse the Curse

Part 1
Take a bolt off of The Chair

How
Part A (Tonight)
1. Write instructions for everyone in the class

Part B (Thursday)
1. Pass out instructions
2. Examine The Chair and find the bolt (also see if I will need any tools)
3. Get all supplies ready
4. Wrap the gift

Part C (Friday)

1. Bring all supplies to school
2. Pass gift to Sam
***3. DISTRACTION ACTION begins at exactly 11:47 A.M.!
4. Meet back at Katie's house after school

"I think it's a great plan," Addy said. "I'm just not sure that I can do it." She slid the pencil under the big clip on the board.

"Why not?" Sam asked.

"Because I don't think that I'm, ya know, talky enough to go around explaining the instructions and asking for everyone's help."

Sam looked at the plan. "I think you can do it, Addy," he said. "I really do. But if you don't want to, then I'll do that part for you."

"Thanks, Sam."

In less than sixteen hours, Part 1 of the Reverse the Curse Plan would begin.

11:47 A.M.

10

Addy stuck to the plan like gum to the bottom of a desk.

That night, she typed the instructions and printed out one for every kid in the class. She wished she knew how to fold them into triangles, like Katie's notes. But she didn't, so instead she folded them in half and used a ladybug sticker to seal each one shut.

The next morning, she handed the instructions to Sam. Sam made sure everyone in the class got one and knew what they were for.

Ms. Stern didn't suspect a thing.

So far, so good, Addy thought.

Next, she examined The Chair. In no time at all, Addy found four bolts. They were underneath, holding the seat in place. Each bolt had six sides, like the crackers she floated in soup. One bolt, the front right, looked loose. *The correct piece*, she thought to herself. She was sure of it. That front right bolt was the *correct piece*.

At lunch, Addy asked Katie to come sit with her and Sam. "The plan is going great," she told them. "The instructions are all handed out, and I found the *correct* bolt."

Addy saw Sam's eyes dart to the right.

"DUCK!" he yelled.

Addy did, but not fast enough. She got hit with four instruction-balls. They were crumpled pieces of paper, the shape and size of a snowball, made of the instructions Addy had printed up and Sam had given out.

"Looks like it's *snowing* in here," Brittney called from her end of the table. She laughed, and three of her instruction-ball-making friends laughed along with her. "Maybe you should build a *fort*, Addy," she went on.

Addy felt the lump in her throat, the cry in her eye.

"Ignore her," Katie said. "She's just a mean bully."

"I know. I'm trying to, but it's hard," Addy replied. "And I need *everyone* in the class to help out tomorrow. If Brittney doesn't, it may not work."

"Let's cross our fingers that she doesn't ruin it for us," Katie said. She picked up the instruction-balls and tossed them into the garbage.

After school Addy continued with the plan and gathered her supplies. First, she looked at the tools hanging on the pegboard in the garage. Her mom was the organized type, so the tools were grouped, labeled, and hung in size order. Addy wasn't sure what size the bolt was, though, so she guessed and took two wrenches that looked about right. Each wrench had two hexagon-shaped openings, one on each end. She hoped one of those four openings would fit.

Next, she swung by the kitchen and pulled a sandwich bag from the box.

After the kitchen Addy went up to her room and took Katie's rubber gloves out of her drawer. Finally, she dug out an old gift, a pin she never liked, and wrapped it up extra, extra tight.

Addy put everything in the front pocket of her backpack. And she was good to go for Part C of the plan. It would be the hardest part, the most important part, and, Addy knew, the part Brittney might spoil.

Friday morning. 11:45. Fifteen minutes until the lunch bell rang. Addy coughed two short coughs. That was the code. It meant: *Get ready, get set . . .*

"MPD," Ms. Stern announced, the same way she did every morning at 11:45. She raised the giant sheet of paper on the corner easel to reveal the Math Problem of the Day. Then she read it aloud, same as always. "In Peter's Pet Store, there were ten parakeets, fifteen parrots, six lovebirds, fourteen canaries, and three cockatoos at the beginning of the week. Peter sold seven parakeets, three parrots, two lovebirds, four canaries, and no cockatoos by the end of the week. How many birds, altogether, did he have left?" She walked back to her desk and added, "Show all of your work in your MPD notebooks. We'll go over the answer after lunch."

Addy's stomach got that wormy feeling. *Now or never*, she thought. She looked at The Chair, which was a vegetable chopping board, four pairs of underwear, and two pairs of sweatpants away from her. *Now. Definitely now.* She stuck the plastic sandwich bag in her pocket and slipped the rubber gloves onto her hands. Then she got the wrenches ready.

11:47. *Cough*, Addy coded. That meant *PART C IS A GO!*

Sam gave her a thumbs-up, looked toward Ms. Stern, and raised his hand.

"What is it, Samuel?"

Sam stood. "Happy birthday!" he exclaimed.

"Excuse me?"

"I said, Happy birthday, Ms. Stern!" Sam smiled and nodded and acted all goofy.

"Today's not my birthday."

"It's not?" Sam looked shocked.

"No. It's not."

Sam stuck his hands in his front pockets and looked down. "I thought *today* was your birthday. And I got the whole class to chip in for something. We were planning to give it to you." Sam looked very disappointed.

If Addy didn't know better, she would have believed the whole thing.

"That's very nice of you, Samuel," Ms. Stern said. "But today's not my birthday."

Sam looked embarrassed. "Is it okay if we *pretend* today is your birthday?" He shrugged a slow, sad shrug and added, "Would *that* be okay?"

Ms. Stern put her pen down and smiled. "Well, I suppose that would be all right."

The plan is working, Addy thought. *Even tough, unfunny teachers like birthday surprises.*

"Great! Thanks!" Sam counted out loud, just the way he was supposed to. On three, everyone got up and gathered around Ms. Stern's desk. Even Brittney. Addy knew Brittney didn't get up because she wanted to help. She got up because she wouldn't miss a chance to look good in front of the teacher. To sing "Happy Birthday" and take part credit for the gift. Just as Sam counted to three again and the whole class called out, "Happy birthday, Ms. Stern," Addy got to work.

She dropped to the ground. With everyone huddled around Ms. Stern's desk, Addy was as invisible as her vegetable chopping board. She got down super-low so she could see the front right bolt under the seat. Right to tighten, left to loosen, she reminded herself. It was a trick her mom had taught her when she had helped change a lightbulb.

"Everyone ready?" Sam asked. Addy saw the back of everyone's head nod. Almost everyone's. Brittney's head stayed put.

Then Addy heard the class sing, "Happy birthday to you . . ."

Addy slipped one of the wrenches around the bolt. It was big and felt jiggly. She turned the wrench around and tried the second opening. It was too big, too. She stuck that wrench in her pocket and pulled the second one out. She tried to put it on the bolt, but it was too small! She turned it around and tried the very last opening. It fit! She turned it left. Easy as anything, the bolt turned. A little loose. Turn. A little more loose.

"Happy birthday to you, happy birthday to you, happy . . ."

Turn. Really loose. Turn. Plink! The bolt fell! It bounced and rolled.

Oh no, *Addy thought. She could not let it get away! She crawled after it.*

". . . birthday to you!" The class cheered and clapped. Then Addy figured Sam was handing Ms. Stern the gift, because he said, "This is from the whole class."

"How nice of all of you," Ms. Stern replied.

Addy lunged after the runaway bolt. She caught it with her gloved hand mid-roll and held on tight.

"Someone did an awfully good wrapping job," Ms. Stern said.

I sure did, Addy thought. She was glad for it, too. She needed the extra time. Addy crawled back to her seat.

"Oh, I think I've got it now."
Addy heard paper rip as Ms. Stern pulled it off the box.

Addy took the plastic bag from her pocket. She dropped the bolt into it, squeezed it shut, and then tucked it and the wrenches safely inside her desk.

"A flower pin. How lovely," Ms. Stern said. "I'll put it on right now, beside my parrot pin."
Sam and Katie made room for Addy to slip in.
Addy tried to look as if she'd been there all along. Tried to smile and breathe normally.
Katie elbowed Addy hard. She pointed her chin to the red-stained gloves still on Addy's hands. The red looked a lot like blood. Addy looked like the bad guy in a scary movie. Her gloved hands were right across the desk from Ms. Stern.
"It *is* a lovely pin," Katie announced, loud and clear.

Everyone turned to her. They weren't used to hearing her sound so unquiet.

Katie stepped smack in front of Addy to pretend to get a closer look at Ms. Stern's gift. With Katie blocking, Addy pulled the gloves off and shoved them up her sleeve.

"What type of flower is it?" Ms. Stern asked. Everyone shook their heads.

"Um, we're not sure," Sam answered.

Addy was sure. She was one thousand percent sure what type of flower that was. One million percent sure of the embarrassing name that flower had to go by. But she sure wasn't telling.

"Well, whatever type of flower it is, it's quite beautiful," Ms. Stern said. "Thank you, class. Thank you all very much."

"*You're welcome, Ms. Stern,*" Brittney replied.

Sam and Katie and about five other kids all gave Addy quiet low-fives as she went back to her desk. It made her feel great. Almost as great as she felt when she walked into Katie's room later that day with the *correct piece* in her hand.

In the battle of Addy vs. The Chair, Addy felt like she had just taken the lead.

Like maybe The Chair should start being scared of The Addy.

Five-Two, Two-Five

11

"Guess what, guys," Addy said.

"What?" Sam asked.

Addy smiled big. "I figured out the next instruction."

"Seriously?" Sam asked. "You know what *change its direction to make it an opposite* means?"

"Uh-huh," Addy answered. She opened her backpack and pulled out two books. They were Jon's Chair books that she had borrowed from Katie. "Last night I studied these really hard," she began. "They're both science books, so I kept asking myself why *these* books. I mean, when I was in Jon's room, I saw about a million science books. So there had to be a reason why he was using mostly these books when he was trying to figure out The Chair."

"He did use those books a lot," Katie said.

"So I read and read, and mostly it was boring. But then I saw the words *change direction* in this book on magnets." She held up Jon's magnet book. "So I read all about magnets, and I realized that it made sense."

"What made sense?" Sam asked.

"We have to magnetize the bolt," Addy answered. "That means make it a magnet," she explained.

"Wait. So direction *two* is still talking about the correct piece from direction *one*?" Katie held up the bag with the bolt in it.

"Uh-huh. Definitely," Addy said. She put the books down. "See, The Bad Luck Chair is filled with bad luck," Addy explained. "Instruction number one told us to take a piece of the bad luck off of it. Instruction two tells us to change its direction and make it an opposite. When you magnetize something," she went on, "you *change the direction* of the particles inside of it. You line them all up so they're facing one way. Before you magnetize it, the particles are facing all different ways. So, in a way, you're making it the *opposite* of what it was." She held up the bag with the bolt in it. "This bolt will become The Good Luck Bolt."

"I didn't really get the whole magnet thing," Sam said. "But you just sounded *for real*, smart."

"I did?"

"*Way,*" Katie agreed.

Addy smiled. "The book even explained *how* to make

something into a magnet," she went on. "And we already have everything we need to do it."

"We do?" Sam asked.

"Uh-huh. It's all that stuff in Jon's shoe box!" Addy got the box from Katie's closet and took out the battery, the wire, and the thin paper. "This is all I need to make the bolt into a magnet," she said.

"Is it hard to do?" Sam asked.

"What? Make a magnet? It's a piece of cake," Addy answered.

Katie tilted her head and said, "Hmmm. Soooo . . ."

Addy could tell she was thinking out loud.

"So you took the bolt off The Chair and you're going to make it into a magnet," Katie said. "Then do you think you have to put it back on The Chair?" she asked. "I mean, can changing this little bolt into a Good Luck Bolt reverse the curse of The Bad Luck Chair?" She held up the bag with the bolt in it.

"I *wish*," Addy answered. "But there are more instructions. That was only number two. There has to be more to it than that."

"What's number three?" Sam asked.

Addy took the folded paper out of her pocket and read number three out loud. "Keep it close."

"The bolt again?" Katie wondered. "Keep it close to what?"

Addy stared straight ahead, deep in thought. Her hand

held tight to her ladybug necklace. "Keep it close," she said softly. She slid the ladybug charm back and forth, back and forth. "Hmmm. Keep it close," she said again. "KEEP IT CLOSE!" she screamed.

"You know what it means?" Sam asked.

"It means that I have to keep the bolt, the magnetized bolt, close to me," she said. "The same way I wear this necklace for good luck, I have to wear the bolt. I'm sure of it. The Good Luck Bolt will protect me from The Bad Luck Chair!"

"Forever?" Sam asked. "It will protect you from The Bad Luck Chair forever?"

Addy thought about Sam's question. "No, not forever, because the bolt won't stay magnetized forever. I just know how to make it a magnet for a short time. And anyway," Addy added, "reversing the curse was supposed to be for everyone, not just for me."

Katie nodded. "*Way*," she said. "Jon needs it to be reversed for *him*, too."

"I know," Addy said softly. She thought a little more

and then added, "The instructions are all about reversing the curse. So the bolt will probably only protect me *during* the reverse."

"But Addy," Sam said. He blinked twice. "That must mean that reversing the curse is a dangerous thing to do. I mean, if you need to be *protected*."

"What do you think can happen?" Katie asked.

"I don't know," Addy answered. "But look, Jon's other book is on natural disasters. Like earthquakes and twisters and hailstorms." She held that book up.

"So you think you could be swallowed up by the earth or sucked into a twister or hit on the head with a giant piece of hail?" Sam asked. He shook himself out like a dog that had just come in from the rain. "I'm getting so porcupine," he added.

"I hope not!" Addy answered. She put her elbows on her knees and her head in her hands. "I don't want to be sucked into a twister!"

Katie looked at the bolt, the materials in the shoe box, and the list. "I don't think you will," she said. "I mean, it seems like half of these instructions have something to do with the bolt, right? So Jon was careful to make sure the reverse would be safe."

Addy agreed, but still, she was scared. "Are you sure?" she asked Katie.

"No, I'm not sure," Katie answered. "But I trust Jon. If you met him you'd trust him, too. He's *careful*."

Addy and Sam were quiet.

"Maybe we should take a break for a while," Katie suggested. "When you said 'piece of cake' before, I sort of got in the mood for cake. I think we have some in the kitchen."

When they were done with their snack, they went back to Katie's room and didn't talk anymore about hail or twisters or earthquakes. Instead, they concentrated on instruction number four.

At time of birth, birthday backwards, set Chair in sight of water and sit.

"Actually," Addy began, "the first part of this one seems easy. It must mean the time *I* was born," she said. "Which was 12:01 P.M."

"Yup," Katie agreed. "And if it means *your* time of birth," she said, "it probably means *your* birthday also."

"May second," Addy replied. "My birthday's May second."

They sat quietly, trying to figure out what a backwards birthday could be.

"What is May *backwards*?" Katie asked. "Hmmm. *Yam!* You think instruction number four has something to do with yams?"

"You mean like sweet potatoes?" Sam asked.

Katie nodded. "Yup. Like sweet potatoes. I love them mashed, with marshmallows cooked on top. Yum."

"No," Addy said, shaking her head. "I don't think yams have anything to do with it."

They sat and thought a while longer.

Addy gasped. "What's today's date?"

"It's Friday, February second," Sam answered. "How come?"

Addy gasped again. "No one panic!" she shouted, jumping to her feet. "But the reverse has to take place this coming Monday!"

"Monday?" Sam asked. "Why Monday?"

"I was born on May second," Addy explained. "Five-two. That, backwards, is two-five. February fifth. Monday!"

"As in today, tomorrow, Sunday, *Monday*?" Katie asked.

"As in."

Katie jumped to her feet and checked the dates on her calendar.

Sam blinked.

And Addy locked her eyes on the next part of instruction number four and repeated it over and over and over. *Set Chair in sight of water and sit. Set Chair in sight of water and sit. Set Chair in sight of water and sit.*

"What water?" she asked out loud. "What water is in sight of The Chair?"

"The closest water to Brookside is the brook," Katie answered. "But you can't see the brook from the school. The fence and trees block it."

"Maybe there's a break in the fence or something," Addy tried. "A spot we never noticed."

"Could be," Sam agreed.

Addy stood up and made an announcement. "I think we should go back to Brookside right now and look for the spot that's *in sight* of the water. And," she continued, "since there's not much time between now and Monday, maybe we should call the other sitters and see if they can help us."

"Yup," Katie said. "We should. I'll get the phone book from the kitchen so we can look up their numbers," she added.

"Want me to do the calling, Addy?" Sam asked. "I know you don't like to."

"Thanks, Sam," Addy answered. "But I'm okay with Ben and Olivia. They're really nice. Maybe you could call Troy and Lucy for me?"

Addy called Ben and Olivia first. She was nervous, because she had never called either of them on the phone before. She explained everything, and both of them said they'd be at the school in ten minutes, no problem. Olivia also told Addy that Lucy had moved away, but she was pretty sure Troy would help.

Sam called Troy. Addy listened as Sam introduced himself and explained what was going on. She thought Sam was really good at stuff like that. He might have been a scaredy-cat some of the time, but when he needed to, Sam could be pretty brave also.

In nine and a half minutes, Addy, Sam, and Katie, plus Ben, Olivia, and Troy, were all in the schoolyard by Brookside. They began to hunt for a spot *in sight of water.*

It was cold and windy, and it was starting to get late. Addy walked up and down the field, peeking, checking. But she could not see the water.

"Hey, everyone," Sam called. He stood on top of the slide. "I can see the water from up here!" Instantly Addy knew that *that* was the spot. That *that* was where Jon had stood when he took all of those pictures. She even remembered the exact one that looked over the fence toward the water.

The platform where kids waited their turn to go down the yellow slide to the blue padded ground—that was where The Chair would have to be on Monday, February 5, at exactly 12:01 P.M. And, as the instruction explained, she would have to be sitting in it.

Everyone gathered at the bottom of the slide.

"Sam! You found it!" Addy clapped for him.

Sam took a bow from the top. He looked shivery.

"Why don't we try to figure out numbers five and six back at Katie's house?" Addy called up to him. "It's freezing out here."

But Ben, Olivia, and Troy were terrified to go anywhere near "the laboratory," the same way Addy had been before she first went.

"I was scared, too," Addy explained. "But there's nothing to be scared of. It's all just stories. Jon is a regular kid who sat in The Chair, just like us. And his room is a regular room. Anyway, we'll be in Katie's room." She paused and then added, "Please come. I really need your help."

Finally they said okay, they'd come. Addy was glad. And proud. She had spoken up, and they had listened.

Once they were all nice and warm in Katie's room, they got back to work on the rest of the instructions.

"*Surround it by forty-two and spin, by way of hand—two times for each plus one time reversed to equal thirteen,*" Addy read out loud.

"Sounds confusing," Ben said. "All those numbers."

Katie patted him on the back.

"Surround it by forty-two what?" Olivia asked. "Pebbles, marbles, cookies? It could be forty-two anythings."

Addy closed her eyes and tried to picture herself in the seat of The Chair, on top of the slide. She tried to see what was around her. But no matter how tightly she shut her eyes, all she kept seeing were the people who were around her in Katie's room. "People?" she tried. "Forty-two people?"

"How are you going to find forty-two people to surround The Chair when there are only twenty-two kids in our class?" Sam asked.

"Wait!" Addy said. "Twenty-two minus me, because I'll be *in* The Chair, is twenty-one."

And then all at once, everyone except Ben screamed, "Twenty-one times two is forty-two!"

"What do we all have two of?" Sam asked.

"Eyes, nostrils, elbows!" Troy called out.

"Ears, knees, hands!" Ben tried.

"Hands!" Addy repeated. "I have to be surrounded by twenty-one people, all connected by their forty-two hands!"

"That makes so much sense," Katie called out. "Because then we can hold hands and *spin* around you in a circle, like in ring around the rosy."

"I can see it!" Addy called out, her eyes shut tight. "I can see it!"

"By way of hand," Ben continued. He held up both of his hands and asked, "Addy, are you a righty or a lefty?"

"Lefty!" she answered, her eyes still shut.

"So they'll spin around you to the left, um, how many times?" Ben asked.

Addy smiled. She knew the answer. It was the same gut feeling she had had from the very beginning when Ben and Olivia were on her porch. "Two times for each of the sitters," she answered. "Me and Jon, plus the four sitters between us. That's six. Two times six equals twelve times."

"Plus one time reversed," Troy added. "So one circle to the right."

"Which makes thirteen," Katie finished. "Exactly what it's supposed to be."

Addy opened her eyes. She knew she was almost there. But then she went blank. No matter how hard she tried, no matter how hard everyone tried to help her, she could not figure out the very last instruction.

Count up to the number between, find the right rhyme, and scream!

"It has to do with words," she said. "Not numbers or

places or dates like some of the other instructions. That's why I'm stuck."

"Then let's skip it for now," Katie suggested. "Instead, we should all work out a new plan for Monday."

Addy agreed. "I think you're right," she said. "Because now that I know what one through five mean, I have to figure out how I'm going to do it."

Forty-nine hours, seven brainstorms, four cheese pizzas, and two batches of brownies later, everything was set. Addy, Sam, and Katie, plus Ben, Olivia, and Troy worked out how, exactly, Addy would go about reversing the curse. It was late Sunday, so there was no time to write notes, print them, and hand them out like the last time. For the plan to work, every kid in the class would need to be called. Addy took the class list from Katie and sat next to the phone in the den. She looked at the names and numbers, then took a few deep breaths.

"Addy," Sam said. "I know you don't like calling people you don't know well. But it's not hard. Really."

Addy nodded.

"If you want me to do it for you, I will. But I think that you can do it, Addy."

"I'm the one reversing the curse," she replied. "I'm the one who needs the help. So I should be the one calling everyone to ask for it. But," she said, "I don't want to do it all by myself." Addy looked at Sam and Katie. "Would you mind sitting here with me while I make the calls?"

Katie and Sam said that of course they would stay with her.

Ben, Olivia, and Troy left. Addy thanked them for coming and told them how, in a tiny way, she was glad that she had sat in The Chair. "I got to meet all of you," she explained.

They agreed, wished her good luck, and said they'd see her tomorrow.

Then Addy got to work. She thought she'd do an easy call first. "Melissa's at my table," she said. "I'll start with her." She dialed the number.

"Hi, is Melissa there?" she asked. "It's Addison Darby, from school." She looked at Sam and smiled.

Addy thought Melissa was really nice. Melissa said she'd be happy to help. That she would do anything to help break that horrible curse.

Next came Hillary. Addy thought Hillary was really nice, too.

Addy looked at the list to pick her next call. "You're right," she said to Sam. "This *isn't* so hard."

"I told you so," he replied.

But then Addy called Emily, one of Brittney's friends.

"Hi, this is Addy, from school."

"Oh. Hi," Emily replied.

"I'm going to try to reverse the curse of The Bad Luck Chair tomorrow," Addy said.

"So?"

"Uh, so I kinda want to tell you how and ask if you could help."

"I don't really believe in The Bad Luck Chair. Brittney doesn't, either."

"You don't?"

"No."

"But will you help me, anyway?" Addy asked.

"Why should I? I don't think a chair can give you bad luck."

"Oh."

"Bye," Emily said.

"Wait—Emily?"

"What?" Emily answered.

"If you don't think that it gives bad luck, then I'll get there early tomorrow and switch chairs with you. Okay? That way I don't have to go through the whole reverse."

"No, that's not okay. You *better not* switch our chairs."

"Why not? If The Chair doesn't scare you, then what's the big deal?"

There was a pause.

"Fine. Maybe I'll help you."

"Thanks, Emily. Here's the plan." Addy explained the whole thing to her.

Sam and Katie high-fived Addy after she hung up.

"You were *so* good," Sam said.

"I can't believe I said those things," Addy replied.

Addy spent the next hour making calls. Most of the

class *wanted* to help. Some didn't seem to care one way or the other but said they'd help her anyway. But a few kids, like Brittney's friends, wouldn't say for sure. They said they'd think about it.

Brittney was the only call left to make.

Addy just couldn't get herself to do it.

"Please, Sam, could you call her? She's *so mean* to me."

Sam dialed her number.

Addy listened to Sam's side of the conversation.

"Hi. This is Sam, from school. Is Brittney there? . . . Oh, hi, Brittney. It didn't sound like you. Anyway, Addy is going to try to reverse the curse of The Bad Luck Chair tomorrow and . . . What? . . . But she needs everyone to help with the . . . Brittney, come on. Brit—Brittney? . . . Brittney? . . . Are you there?"

Sam blinked, then hung up the phone. "She's *really* mean," he said.

"She's not going to help, is she?" Addy asked.

Sam shook his head. "I don't think so."

"She could ruin the whole thing," Addy said.

"But we have Ben and Olivia as backups," Sam replied. "They have the same lunch period, so they can help us out. If only one kid is absent or at the nurse or someplace else, we're still okay."

There was nothing for Addy to do now but wait for tomorrow. Two-Five.

If everything went right, The Chair would be history.

If anything went wrong, Addy would be.

Reverse the Curse

12

P. Addison Darby was about to reverse the curse of The Brookside Elementary Bad Luck Chair.

Or get crushed by giant hail or swallowed by an earthquake or sucked into a twister trying.

She walked into Room 36 feeling gutsy and game. She was ready. Scared, but ready.

"Go for it, Addy," one kid whispered to her.

"Good luck," another kid said.

"You're braver than me," Melissa told her.

And then Addy heard laughter. She turned and saw that it was Brittney and her three mean friends. They were all looking right at her.

"Addy's scared of her chair," Brittney said to them. "Next she'll be scared of her desk. And then maybe her pencil, too!" They all laughed.

Addy did her best to ignore them. She looked away and got ready for her day.

The morning went about as fast as a slug crossing the sidewalk. Finally it was 11:45, and Ms. Stern revealed the MPD. "A flock of geese flew by," she read. "The first row had only one goose. Each row after that had twice as many geese as the row before it. There were twelve rows. How many geese flew by in all?"

Addy took out her notebook and pretended to work. Instead, she went over the plan one last time in her head. She had memorized it like it was the biggest test she would ever study for. She knew even one small mistake could blow the whole thing.

With two kids absent, the classroom count was at 19. Olivia and Ben would bring the count back up to 21. But if Brittney and her friends didn't help, Addy would be in trouble. She needed 21 kids and 42 hands to reverse the curse of The Bad Luck Chair.

She watched the clock.

11:51.

11:52.

11:52 and 30 seconds.

11:53. Katie gave Addy a thumbs-up. Sam turned to her and mouthed, "You sure you want to do this?" Addy nodded yes, put Katie's gloves on, then slipped The Good Luck Bolt around her neck. It dangled right next to her ladybug.

Addy was ready.

And the final part of the Reverse the Curse Plan began.

"Ms. Stern!" Sam called.

Ms. Stern looked up from her desk. "Yes?"

"I just saw a bird fly by in the hall!"

Ms. Stern looked toward the door. "A bird? Inside the school?"

"Yuh-huh. I think maybe it was a sparrow."

"Really?" Ms. Stern got up and peeked out the square window on the classroom door.

"I'm not positively sure, but I think it was a baby," Sam added.

"Poor thing." Ms. Stern opened the door. She stuck her head out and looked up the hall, then down.

Addy was worried. It wasn't working. Ms. Stern was still *in* the room.

"I think maybe it was hurt or something," Sam called out. "Its wing looked funny."

That did it. Ms. Stern stepped out of the room. "Everyone, keep working on the MPD," she called.

Melissa's part came next. She took a toilet-seat liner out of her desk.

"I can't believe you're doing this," Addy heard Brittney say to Melissa. "It's so immature."

Melissa paused, glanced at The Chair, and replied, "That *thing* really scares me, Brittney." Then Melissa got up and walked out the door to where Ms. Stern stood. "I have to use the bathroom," she said, waving the liner around. "It's sort of an emergency."

"Go ahead," Ms. Stern replied.

Melissa walked down the hall toward the girls' room. When she was about halfway there, she stopped. "Ms. Stern," she called, "I just heard a tweet somewhere around here."

Ms. Stern walked to where Melissa stood.

Addy turned to Eric Zyber. He sat in the seat closest to the last window. She nodded at him and mouthed, "Go!"

Eric slid out of his seat and moved the cactus, the bean plant, and the snail tank away from that last window. Then he hopped up onto the sill, unlocked the latch, and slid it way up.

Cold air rushed in.

It was finally Addy's turn. She stood and hid the vegetable chopping board under her MPD notebook. Then, with her gloved hands, she lifted The Chair and carried it across the back of the room.

"Everyone working on the MPD?" Ms. Stern called, her head and one shoulder popping back in.

Addy dropped to the ground. She ducked behind Eric. The Chair stood behind Eric's chair.

She held her breath and stayed perfectly still. She didn't dare move even an eyelash.

Maybe it was the angle of the door.

Maybe it was Ms. Stern's concern for a baby bird.

Maybe it was that Addy had scrunched herself up to the size of a salami.

No one in Room 36 was sure how, but a miracle had happened. Ms. Stern had *not* seen that The Chair was not by Addy's desk. She had *not* seen that Addy was not in The Chair. Just as she was about to turn back around, Brittney called, "Ms. Stern?"

Addy knew she was Done. She would not get to finish what Jon had begun. The curse would never be reversed. Show over.

"Yes, Brittney?"

"THERE'S THE BIRD!" Sam yelled. He stood up and pointed out the door. "Ms. Stern! There's the bird! It just flew right past you! Didn't you see it?"

Ms. Stern swung around. She was frantic, looking this way, then that way.

Addy sprang back up. She lifted The Chair, set it on the empty sill, and jumped up there with it. She held it tight and lowered it out the window. It was heavy, but Addy was so shook-up, she felt like she could have lifted and lowered a truck out that window. When The Chair was on the ground outside, Addy slid the window down. Then she and Eric put everything back just the way it was.

As she returned to her desk, Addy took the gloves off and stuck them in her pocket. She and The Chair were enemies, but they were in this together. She felt like it was time to get rid of anything between them. No gloves, no toilet-seat liners, no nothing.

It was Addy vs. The Chair.

With The Chair out the window, Addy had to fake-sit. She would have to stay like that until the bell rang. Which, if everything went as planned, would be a little earlier than usual. She had practiced fake-sitting at home. If she leaned her elbows on the desk, she was pretty sure she could hang in there long enough.

Ms. Stern and Melissa came back into the room. Ms. Stern said, "I didn't see a bird."

Sam shrugged. "Maybe it found its way out the same way it got in."

"Maybe," Ms. Stern replied, one eyebrow up.

Addy saw Brittney turn around and look at her. Brittney locked her eyes on Addy and stared. She smiled her mean smile. Addy could tell that Brittney liked watching her struggle to fake-sit. But Brittney's stare and mean smile actually gave Addy the jolt she needed to stay put.

Addy's legs burned. She pushed her weight from one side to the other, then leaned forward and tried to rest mostly on her elbows. Soon every muscle began to feel like cooked spaghetti.

"Hang in there, Addy," Melissa whispered.

"You can do it," Hillary mouthed.

The minute hand moved.

It was 11:58. Two minutes before the lunch bell *usually* rang. *Please*, Addy thought. *Please ring now.*

Brrrrring.

"Put your MPD notebooks away. We'll go over the problem after lunch."

The kids in Room 36 tore out. Ms. Stern tried to slow them down, but it was no use. They had to be in a circle around the slide before 12:01. Plus, they had to be back in the cafeteria before any of the lunch ladies noticed that Room 36's table was empty.

Addy ran out of the building, then back around to where her classroom was. She was freezing. No one had taken a coat because no one was supposed to be outside.

When she got to The Chair, she saw Ms. Stern through the window. Which meant that if Ms. Stern looked out, she would see Addy. With no time to wait for her to get up and go to the faculty room, Addy got down and crawled. She grabbed The Chair and dragged it away.

Addy's bare hands had touched The Chair. There was no turning back.

As soon as Addy was far enough from the window, she got to her feet, picked The Chair up, and ran wildly toward the slide. Her legs felt rubbery from her fake sit, and her hands stung from the cold.

Addy ran across a patch of icy snow and slid. She tried to catch herself, but her foot tangled with a Chair leg and The Chair fell from her hands. It tumbled ahead of her. Addy couldn't stop, and she flew over it!

Addy and The Chair both landed flat on their backs on the frozen ground.

"You alive?" Sam asked as Addy opened her eyes. She saw him and Katie standing over her.

"I think so."

"Then get up!" Katie shouted. "This is just The Chair fighting back. You can beat it. You're almost there!" Katie pulled Addy's shoulders up, and Sam grabbed her hands and got her to her feet. Addy picked The Chair back up and ran as fast as her jittery feet would go. Katie and Sam ran right alongside her. As she got close to the slide, a circle of kids opened up so she could run right in. Addy put the back of The Chair over her arm so it rested inside her elbow. She climbed the ladder, and with each step up the Chair smacked the side of her knee. When she finally made it to the top, she plunked The Chair down on the platform and dropped into it.

It was exactly 12:01.

From her spot high on the slide, Addy could see Olivia and Ben running toward her. She could also see Brittney and her three friends leaning on the monkey bars, just a few steps away from the slide.

"Brittney, get into the circle!" Sam yelled. "Hurry!"

"Like I might *ever*," Brittney called back and laughed. Then she added, "We're just here to watch a bunch of two-year-olds dance in a circle around a slide. We thought we'd get a good laugh out of it."

Addy felt her heart beat fast. She felt her bones shake.

"It'll only take a minute," Sam yelled back. "Come on. We need your help. Get in!"

"Why?" Brittney asked. "Addy already sat in doody. Who cares where she sits next?"

Addy listened as Brittney and her friends laughed. She looked at where she was and thought about why she was there and in that blink of time everything, *every single thing* she had ever wanted to say to Brittney but didn't have the guts to say was right there, in her mouth. "Brittney!" she yelled. "YOU'RE JUST A BIG BULLY! You make yourself feel good by making other people feel bad!" Addy trembled all over. What she had said scared her. But it also made her feel strong.

"Addy sat in doody, Addy sat in doody," Brittney sang. She looked at her friends, but they didn't sing along.

"If *you* sat in The Chair," Addy screamed, "and *you* needed help, I would've helped you!"

Brittney laughed. "I'm not scared of a chair like you are," she answered. "So I would never have needed your help."

Addy stood up, and from high on the slide she looked down at Brittney. She felt big and brave and she didn't care if the kids in her class were staring at her. "*You* may not be scared of The Chair," Addy yelled, "but other people are! It hurt Katie's brother, Jon. And Ben. And Olivia. Plus a lot of other kids, too." And then Addy said what she had really wanted to say all along. "It doesn't matter what you think of The Chair. It matters that you're too *mean* even to help someone who needs your help. You're *mean*, Brittney. You're the *meanest* person I've ever met!"

There was silence. Addy had said everything she wanted to say. Even though she was just on top of the slide, she felt like she was on top of the world.

"Get into the circle!" Sam yelled. "Quick," he added, checking his watch. "We're running out of time!"

Brittney's friends moved away from her and stood with all of the other kids around the slide.

"Hey! Get back here!" she called to them.

"It's not such a big deal, Brittney," one of them answered. "It'll just take a minute to help."

"Get in the circle, Brittney!" Addy screamed.

And Brittney finally joined the others. There were 21 kids and 42 hands.

Addy felt for the bolt around her neck and held it close. She watched the ground for earthquakes and the sky for hail and twisters. "Hold hands and circle twelve times to the left!" she called out.

As the class moved to the left, Addy was sure she could feel something. She wasn't sure what, but something.

Everyone picked up speed to keep warm. The faster they spun, the more it all looked like a cartoon blur to Addy. In the spin of color and cold air, Addy felt it more and more. It was powerful, tremendous, right there in her face, yet unseen.

It was the *energy*!

Sam kept count and called out the laps. "Ten! Eleven!"

"One more to go!" Addy yelled.

The energy swelled, the wind picked up, and Addy held tight to the seat of The Chair with one hand and tight to the bolt with the other.

"Twelve!" Sam called out.

"Now circle one time to the right!" Addy screamed.

The energy was so strong that the air smelled electrical and seemed to turn a greenish orange.

Everyone moved to the right.

The sky rumbled. It sounded like a deep, angry growl. Addy squeezed the bolt as hard as she could. "One, two, three, four!" she called out. Then she tilted her face toward the sky and with all of her heart screamed out, "THIS CHAIR WILL GIVE BAD LUCK NO MORE!"

As the last sound left her mouth and touched the air, everything became still.

The wind calmed. The sky quieted. The air felt crisp and looked clear.

And The Chair, The Brookside Elementary Bad Luck Chair, was suddenly nothing more than an ordinary chair.

The Party

13

Later that day, the day that would forever be known in Brookside Elementary as The Curse Reverse Day, Katie threw a party. She invited the whole class, plus Ben, Olivia, Troy, and her big brother, Jon. The party was to celebrate that the curse had been broken. After years and years of kids being afraid of finding The Chair parked by their desks, they could finally feel safe to sit.

Addy stood on the third step from the bottom of the stairs that led to Katie's basement. She wore one purple shoelace and one green one. Katie had given them to her as a curse-reverse gift. "Thank you, everyone," she called out. "Thanks for coming to Katie's party. And thanks for all of your help. I wouldn't have been able to reverse the curse without it." Kids cheered and clapped.

"And thanks especially to my *two* best friends, Sam and

Katie," Addy went on. "Even when I was having all that bad luck, I was very lucky to have both of you."

Sam nodded and gave Addy a fake punch on the shoulder. Katie smiled so wide the whole room felt like smiling, too.

"And also, uh, thanks, Brittney. Thanks for finally helping me out."

Brittney looked a little limp. Sort of like a beach ball with some of the air let out.

"Jon!" Katie screamed.

Jonathan Odayo came down the steps. It was the very first time Addy had actually seen him. She had pictured him to be big and scary and unlucky-looking. But he wasn't any of those things. Jon looked nice.

"Are you coming to the party?" Katie asked him.

"Nah," he answered. "But I just wanted to tell you that whatever you did, it worked. I have scientific proof."

"You do?" Katie asked.

"I do." Jon stuck his hand in his coat pocket and said, "I went over to SuperShop Grocery just now and put a quarter in the gum-ball machine there. Guess what happened." Before Katie could answer, he pulled two green gum balls from his pocket. "Two came out! I was hoping for one. But TWO GREEN GUM BALLS dropped right into my hand! Plus," he shouted, "I GOT MY QUARTER BACK!"

The kids went crazy! Addy and Sam high-fived Katie and Jon. Then Jon disappeared back up the steps.

Everyone sat on the floor, listening to music, eating chips, and drinking soda.

"I have two questions," Melissa said to Addy.

"What?"

"The first one is, how did you get The Chair back into the room?"

"I carried it there," Addy answered. "Ms. Stern had already left for lunch, and the door wasn't locked. So I just put it back. What's the second question?"

"How'd you get the bell to ring two minutes early?"

"Yeah, I was wondering that, too," a few kids called out. "How'd you do that?"

"Easy," Addy answered. "I got to school early today and told Mrs. Hibbard, the nice lady in the office, all about The Chair and the curse reverse. And I asked her if she could help me out by ringing the bell a little early so we could all be on the back field in time. I kinda knew she would, because she was so nice about changing my name on the class list and . . ."

Addy stopped. But she knew it was too late. She had said too much.

"She changed your name on the class list?" Brittney asked.

Addy nodded. She slid the bolt necklace back and forth, back and forth.

"What do you mean she changed your name?" Brittney went on.

Addy looked around the room and knew there was

nothing to be scared of. "In kindergarten," she began, "Mrs. Hibbard put my middle name, Addison, on the school list as my first name. Because I was embarrassed by my real first name."

"What is it?" Melissa asked.

"My name?"

"Yeah. What's your real first name?"

"It's the name of a flower," Addy answered.

"Rose?" Melissa guessed.

"Daisy?" Brittney tried.

Addy shook her head. "It starts with the letter *P*," she said.

"Petunia?"

"Pansy?"

Again, Addy shook her head.

"Come on, tell us," they all urged.

Feeling gutsy—really, really gutsy—and lucky, too, Addy told her friends her first name. "Pee-oh-nee," she sounded out, loud and clear for them. "My name is Peony."

No one laughed.

No one but Addy. Because right then, right there, Addy felt about as happy and safe as a kid could feel. So she laughed a gushing, giddy laugh of pure joy.

Joy for her new friends.

Joy for her old friends.

And joy for her victory over The Brookside Elementary Bad Luck Chair.